FOR LOVE
OF
IMABELLE

by Chester Himes

THE CHATHAM BOOKSELLER
CHATHAM, NEW JERSEY

Reissued 1973, by The Chatham Bookseller
by arrangement with Chester Himes

Library of Congress No. 73-84808
ISBN 0-911860-33-9

CHAPTER 1

HANK counted the stack of money. It was a lot of money—
a hundred and fifty brand new ten-dollar bills. He looked
at Jackson through cold yellow eyes.

"You give me fifteen C's—right?"

He wanted it straight. It was strictly business.

He was a small, dapper man with mottled brown skin
and thin straightened hair. He looked like business.

"That's right," Jackson said. "Fifteen hundred bucks."

It was strictly business with Jackson too.

Jackson was a short, black, fat man with purple-red
gums and pearly white teeth made for laughing, but Jackson wasn't laughing. It was too serious for Jackson to be
laughing. Jackson was only twenty-eight years old, but it
was such serious business that he looked a good ten years
older.

"You want me to make you fifteen G's—right?" Hank
kept after him.

"That's right," Jackson said. "Fifteen thousand bucks."

He tried to sound happy, but he was scared. Sweat was
trickling from his short kinky hair. His round black face
was glistening like an eight-ball.

"My cut'll be ten percent—fifteen C's—right?"

"That's right. I pays you fifteen hundred bucks for the
deal."

"I take five percent for my end," Jodie said. "That's
seven hundred and fifty. Okay?"

Jodie was a working stiff, a medium-sized, root-colored,
rough-skinned, muscular boy, dressed in a leather jacket
and GI pants. His long, thick hair was straightened on the

5

ends and burnt red, and nappy at the roots where it grew out black. It hadn't been cut since New Year's Eve and this was already the middle of February. One look at Jodie was enough to tell that he was strictly a square.

"Okay," Jackson said. "You gets seven hundred and fifty for your end."

It was Jodie who had got Hank to make all this money for him.

"I gets the rest," Imabelle said.

The others laughed.

Imabelle was Jackson's woman. She was a cushioned-lipped, hot-bodied, banana-skin chick with the speckled-brown eyes of a teaser and the high-arched, ball-bearing hips of a natural-born *amante*. Jackson was as crazy about her as moose for doe.

They were standing around the kitchen table. The window looked out on 142nd Street. Snow was falling on the ice-locked piles of garbage stretching like levees along the gutters as far as the eye could see.

Jackson and Imabelle lived in a room down the hall. Their landlady was at work and the other roomers were absent. They had the place to themselves.

Hank was going to turn Jackson's hundred and fifty ten-dollar bills into a hundred and fifty hundred-dollar bills.

Jackson watched Hank roll each bill carefully into a sheet of chemical paper, stick the roll into a cardboard tube shaped like a firecracker, and stack the tubes in the oven of the new gas stove.

Jackson's eyes were red with suspicion.

"You sure you're using the right paper?"

"I ought to know it. I made it," Hank said.

Hank was the only man in the world who possessed the chemically treated paper that was capable of raising the denomination of money. He had developed it himself.

Nevertheless Jackson watched Hank's every move. He even studied the back of Hank's head when Hank turned to put the money into the oven.

"Don't you be so worried, Daddy," Imabelle said, putting her smooth yellow arm about his black-coated shoulder. "You know it can't fail. You saw him do it before."

Jackson had seen him do it before, true enough. Hank had given him a demonstration two days before. He had turned a ten into a hundred right before Jackson's eyes. Jackson had taken the hundred to the bank. He had told the clerk he had won it shooting dice and had asked the clerk if it was good. The clerk had said it was as good as if it had been made in the mint. Hank had had the hundred changed and had given Jackson back his ten. Jackson knew that Hank could do it.

But this time it was for keeps.

That was all the money Jackson had in the world. All the money he'd saved in the five years he'd worked for Mr. H. Exodus Clay, the undertaker. And that hadn't come easy. He drove the limousines for the funerals, brought in the dead in the pickup hearse, cleaned the chapel, washed the bodies and swept out the embalming room, hauled away the garbage cans of clotted blood, trimmed meat and rotten guts.

All the money he could get Mr. Clay to advance him on his salary. All the money he could borrow from his friends. He'd pawned his good clothes, his gold watch and his imitation diamond stickpin and the gold signet ring he'd found in a dead man's pocket. Jackson didn't want anything to happen.

"I ain't worried," Jackson said. "I'm just nervous, that's all. I don't want to get caught."

"How're we goin' to get caught, Daddy? Ain't nobody got no idea what we're doing here."

Hank closed the oven door and lit the gas.

"Now I make you a rich man, Jackson."

"Thank the Lord. Amen," Jackson said, crossing himself.

He wasn't a Catholic. He was a Baptist, a member of the First Baptist Church of Harlem. But he was a very religious young man. Whenever he was troubled he crossed himself just to be on the safe side.

7

"Set down, Daddy," Imabelle said. "Your knees are shakin'."

Jackson sat down at the table and stared at the stove. Imabelle stood beside him, drew his head tight against her bosom. Hank consulted his watch. Jodie stood to one side, his mouth wide open.

"Ain't it done yet?" Jackson asked.

"Just one more minute," Hank said.

He moved to the sink to get a drink of water.

"Ain't the minute up yet?" Jackson asked.

At that instant the stove exploded with such force it blew the door off.

"Great balls of fire!" Jackson yelled. He came up from his chair as if the seat of his pants had blown up.

"Look out, Daddy!" Imabelle screamed and hugged Jackson so hard she threw him flat on his back.

"Hold it, in the name of the law!" a new voice shouted.

A tall, slim colored man with a cop's scowl rushed into the kitchen. He had a pistol in his right hand and a gold-plated badge in his left.

"I'm a United States marshal. I'm shooting the first one who moves."

He looked as if he meant it.

The kitchen had filled with smoke and stunk like black gunpowder. Gas was pouring from the stove. The scorched cardboard tubes that had been cooking in the oven were scattered over the floor.

"It's the law!" Imabelle screamed.

"I heard him!" Jackson yelled.

"Let's beat it!" Jodie shouted.

He tripped the marshal into the table and made for the door. Hank got there before him and Jodie went out on Jodie's back. The marshal sprawled across the table top.

"Run, Daddy!" Imabelle said.

"Don't wait for me," Jackson replied.

He was on his hands and knees, trying as hard as he could to get to his feet. But Imabelle was running so hard she stumbled over him and knocked him down again as she made for the door.

Before the marshal could straighten up all three of them had escaped.

"Don't you move!" he shouted at Jackson.

"I ain't moving, Marshal."

When the marshal finally got his feet underneath him he yanked Jackson erect and snapped a pair of handcuffs about his wrists.

"Trying to make a fool out of me! You'll get ten years for this."

Jackson turned a battleship gray.

"I ain't done nothing, Marshal. I swear to God."

Jackson had attended a Negro college in the South, but whenever he was excited or scared he began talking in his native dialect.

"Sit down and shut up," the marshal ordered.

He shut off the gas and began picking up the cardboard tubes for evidence. He opened one, took out a brand-new hundred-dollar bill and held it up toward the light.

"Raised from a ten. The markings are still on it."

Jackson had started to sit down but he stopped suddenly and began to plead.

"It wasn't me what done that, Marshal. I swear to God. It was them two fellows who got away. All I done was come into the kitchen to get a drink of water."

"Don't lie to me, Jackson. I know you. I've got the goods on you, man. I've been watching you three counterfeiters for days."

Tears welled up in Jackson's eyes, he was so scared.

"Listen, Marshal, I swear to God I didn't have nothing to do with that. I don't even know how to do it. The little man called Hank who got away is the counterfeiter. He's the only one who's got the paper."

"Don't worry about them, Jackson. I'll get them too. But I've already got you, and I'm taking you down to the Federal Building. So I'm warning you, anything you say to me will be used against you in court."

Jackson slid from the chair and got down on his knees.

"Leave me go just this once, Marshal." The tears began streaming down his face. "Just this once, Marshal. I've

9

never been arrested before. I'm a church man, I ain't dishonest. I confess, I put up the money for Hank to raise, but it was him who was breaking the law, not me. I ain't done nothing wouldn't nobody do if they had a chance to make a pile of money."

"Get up, Jackson, and take your punishment like a man," the marshal said. "You're just as guilty as the others. If you hadn't put up the tens, Hank couldn't have changed them into hundreds."

Jackson saw himself serving ten years in prison. Ten years away from Imabelle. Jackson had only had Imabelle for eleven months, but he couldn't live without her. He was going to marry her as soon as she got her divorce from that man down South she was still married to. If he went to prison for ten years, by then she'd have another man and would have forgotten all about him. He'd come out of prison an old man, thirty-eight years old, dried up. No one would give him a job. No woman would want him. He'd be a bum, hungry, skinny, begging on the streets of Harlem, sleeping in doorways, drinking canned heat to keep warm. Mama Jackson hadn't raised a son for that, struggled to send him through the college for Negroes, just to have him become a convict. He just couldn't let the marshal take him in.

He clutched the marshal about the legs.

"Have mercy on a poor sinner, man. I know I did wrong, but I'm not a criminal. I just got talked into it. My woman wanted a new winter coat, we want to get a place of our own, maybe buy a car. I just yielded to temptation. You're a colored man like me, you ought to understand that. Where are we poor colored people goin' to get any money from?"

The marshal yanked Jackson to his feet.

"God damn it, get yourself together, man. Go take a drink of water. You act as if you think I'm Jesus Christ."

Jackson went to the sink and drank a glass of water. He was crying like a baby.

"You could have a little mercy," he said. "Just a little of the milk of human mercy. I've done lost all my money in

10

this deal already. Ain't that punishment enough? Do I have to go to jail too?"

"Jackson, you're not the first man I've arrested for a crime. Suppose I'd let off everybody. Where would I be then? Out of a job. Broke and hungry. Soon I'd be on the other side of the law, a criminal myself."

Jackson looked at the marshal's hard brown face and mean, dirty eyes. He knew there was no mercy in the man. As soon as colored folks got on the side of the law, they lost all Christian charity, he was thinking.

"Marshal, I'll pay you two hundred dollars if you let me off," he offered.

The marshal looked at Jackson's wet face.

"Jackson, I shouldn't do this. But I can see that you're an honest man, just led astray by a woman. And being as you're a colored man like myself, I'm going to let you off this time. You give me the two hundred bucks, and you're a free man."

The only way Jackson could get two hundred dollars this side of the grave was to steal it from his boss. Mr. Clay always kept two or three thousand dollars in his safe. There was nothing Jackson hated worse than having to steal from Mr. Clay. Jackson had never stolen any money in his life. He was an honest man. But there was no other way out of this hole.

"I ain't got it here. I got it at the funeral parlor where I work."

"Well, that being the case, I'll drive you there in my car, Jackson. But you'll have to give me your word of honor you won't try to escape."

"I ain't no criminal," Jackson protested. "I won't try to escape, I swear to God. I'll just go inside and get the money and bring it out to you."

The marshal unlocked Jackson's handcuffs and motioned him ahead. They went down the four flights of stairs and came out on Eighth Avenue, where the apartment house fronted.

The marshal gestured toward a battered black Ford.

"You can see that I'm a poor man myself, Jackson."

"Yes sir, but you ain't as poor as me, because I've not only got nothing but I've got minus nothing."

"Too late to cry now, Jackson."

They climbed into the car, drove south on 134th Street, east to the corner of Lenox Avenue, and parked in front of the *H. Exodus Clay Funeral Parlor*.

Jackson got out and went silently up the red rubber treads of the high stone steps; entered through the curtained glass doors of the old stone house, and peered into the dimly lit chapel where three bodies were on display in the open caskets.

Smitty, the other chauffeur and handyman, was silently embracing a woman on one of the red, velvet-covered benches similar to the ones on which the caskets stood. He hadn't heard Jackson enter.

Jackson tiptoed past them silently and went down the hall to the broom closet. He got a dust mop and cloth and tiptoed back to the office at the front.

At that time of afternoon, when they didn't have a funeral, Mr. Clay took a nap on the couch in his office. Marcus, the embalmer, was left in charge. But Marcus always slipped out to Small's bar, over on 135th Street and Seventh Avenue.

Silenty Jackson opened the door of Mr. Clay's office, tiptoed inside, stood the dust mop against the wall and began dusting the small black safe that sat in the corner beside an old-fashioned roll-top desk. The door of the safe was closed but not locked.

Mr. Clay lay on his side, facing the wall. He looked like a refugee from a museum, in the dim light from the floor lamp that burned continuously in the front window.

He was a small, elderly man with skin like parchment, faded brown eyes, and long gray bushy hair. His standard dress was a tail coat, double-breasted dove-gray vest, striped trousers, wing collar, black Ascot tie adorned with a gray pearl stickpin, and rimless nose-glasses attached to a long black ribbon pinned to his vest.

"That you, Marcus?" he asked suddenly without turning over.

12

Jackson started. "No sir, it's me, Jackson."

"What are you doing in here, Jackson?"

"I'm just dusting, Mr. Clay," Jackson said, as he eased open the door of the safe.

"I thought you took the afternoon off."

"Yes sir. But I recalled that Mr. Williams' family will be coming tonight to view Mr. Williams' remains, and I knew you'd want everything spic and span when they got here."

"Don't overdo it, Jackson," Mr. Clay said sleepily. "I ain't intending to give you a raise."

Jackson forced himself to laugh.

"Aw, you're just joking, Mr. Clay. Anyway, my woman ain't home. She's gone visiting."

While he was speaking, Jackson opened the inner safe door.

"Thought that was the trouble," Mr. Clay mumbled.

In the money drawer was a stack of twenty-dollar bills, pinned together in bundles of hundreds.

"Ha ha, you're just joking, Mr. Clay," Jackson said as he took out five bundles and stuck them into his side pants-pocket.

He rattled the handle of the dust mop while closing the safe's two doors.

"Lord, you just have to forgive me in this emergency," he said silently, then spoke in a loud voice, "Got to clean the steps now."

Mr. Clay didn't answer.

Jackson tiptoed back to the broom closet, put away the cloth and mop, tiptoed silently back toward the front door. Smitty and the woman were still enjoying life.

Jackson let himself out silently and went down the stairs to the marshal's car. He palmed two of the hundred-dollar bundles and slipped them through the open window to the marshal.

The marshal held them down between his legs while he counted them. Then he nodded and stuck them into his inside coat-pocket.

"Let this be a lesson to you, Jackson," he said. "Crime doesn't pay."

13

CHAPTER 2

As soon as the marshal drove off, Jackson started running. He knew that Mr. Clay would count his money the first thing on awakening. Not because he suspected anybody would steal it. There was always someone on duty. It was just a habit. Mr. Clay counted his money when he went to sleep and when he woke up, when he unlocked his safe and when he locked it. If he wasn't busy, he counted it fifteen to twenty times a day.

Jackson knew that Mr. Clay would begin questioning the help when he missed the five hundred. He wouldn't call in the police until he was dead certain who had stolen his money. That was because Mr. Clay believed in ghosts. Mr. Clay knew damn well if ever the ghosts started collecting the money he'd cheated their relatives out of, he'd be headed for the poor house.

Jackson knew that next Mr. Clay would go to his room searching for him.

He was pressed but not panicked. If the Lord would just give him time enough to locate Hank and get him to raise the three hundred into three thousand, he might be able to slip the money back into the safe before Mr. Clay began suspecting him.

But first he had to get the twenty-dollar bills changed into ten-dollar bills. Hank couldn't raise twenties because there was no such thing as a two-hundred-dollar bill.

He ran down to Seventh Avenue and turned into Small's bar. Marcus spotted him. He didn't want Marcus to see him changing the money. He came in by one door and went out by the other; ran up the street to the Red

Rooster. They only had sixteen tens in the cash register. Jackson took those and started out. A customer stopped him and changed the rest.

Jackson came out on Seventh Avenue and ran down 142nd Street toward home. It came to him, as he was slipping and sliding on the wet icy sidewalks, that he didn't know where to look for Hank. Imabelle had met Jodie at her sister's apartment in the Bronx.

Imabelle's sister, Margie, had told Imabelle that Jodie knew a man who could make money. Imabelle had brought Jodie to talk to Jackson about it. When Jackson said he'd give it a trial, it had been Jodie who'd gotten in touch with Hank.

Jackson felt certain that Imabelle would know where to find Jodie if not Hank. The only thing was, he didn't know where Imabelle was.

He stopped across the street and looked up at the kitchen window to see if the light was on. It was dark. He tried to remember if it was himself or the marshal who'd turned off the light. It didn't make any difference anyway. If the landlady had returned from work she was sure to be in the kitchen raising fifteen million dollars' worth of hell.

Jackson went around to the front of the apartment house and climbed the four flights of stairs. He listened at the front door of the apartment. He didn't hear a sound from inside. He unlocked the door, slipped quietly within. He didn't hear anyone moving about. He tiptoed down to his room and closed himself in. Imabelle hadn't returned.

He wasn't worried about her. Imabelle could take care of herself. But time was pressing him.

While trying to decide whether to wait there or go out and look for her, he heard the front door being unlocked. Someone entered the front hall, closed and locked the door. Footsteps approached. The first hall door was opened.

"Claude," an irritable woman's voice called.

There was no reply. The footsteps crossed the hall. The opposite door was opened.

"Mr. Canefield."

The landlady was calling the roll.

"As evil a woman as God ever made," Jackson muttered. "He must have made her by mistake."

More footsteps sounded. Jackson crawled quickly underneath the bed, keeping his overcoat and hat on. He heard the door being opened.

"Jackson."

Jackson could feel her examining the room. He heard her try to open Imabelle's big steamer-trunk.

"They keeps this trunk locked all the time," she complained to herself. "Him and that woman. Living in sin. And him calls himself a Christian. If Christ knew what kind of Christians He got here in Harlem He'd climb back up on the cross and start over."

Jackson heard her walk back toward the kitchen. He rolled from underneath the bed and got to his feet.

"Merciful Lawd!" he heard her exclaim. "Somebody done blowed up my brand-new stove."

Jackson flung open the door to his room and ran down the hall. He got out of the front door before she saw him. He went upstairs instead of down, taking the stairs two at a time. He had scarcely turned at the landing when he heard the landlady run out into the corridor, chasing him.

"Who you be, you dirty bastard!" she yelled. "It you, Jackson, or Claude? Blew up my stove!"

He came out on the roof and ran to the roof of the adjoining building, past a pigeon cage, and found the door to the stairway unlocked. He went down the stairs like a bouncing ball but stopped at the street doorway to reconnoiter.

The landlady was peering from her doorway in the other building. He drew back his head before she saw him, and watched the sidewalk from an angle.

He saw Mr. Clay's personal Cadillac sedan turn the corner and pull in at the curb. Smitty, the other chauffeur, was driving. Mr. Clay got out and went inside.

Jackson knew they were looking for him. He turned, running, and went through the hallway and out of the back door. There was a small concrete courtyard filled with garbage cans and trash, closed in by high concrete walls. He put a half-filled garbage can against the wall and climbed over, tearing the middle button from his overcoat. He came out in the back courtyard of the building that faced 142nd Street. He ran through the hallway and turned toward Seventh Avenue.

A cruising taxi came in his direction. He hailed it. He'd have to break one of the ten-dollar bills, and that would cost him a hundred dollars, but there was no help for it now. It was just hurry-hurry.

A black boy was driving. Jackson gave him the address of Imabelle's sister in the Bronx. The black boy made a U-turn in the icy street as though he liked skating, and took off like a lunatic.

"I'm in a hurry," Jackson said.

"I'm hurrying, ain't I?" the black boy called over his shoulder.

"But I ain't in no hurry to get to heaven."

"We ain't going to heaven."

"That's what I'm scared of."

The black boy wasn't thinking about Jackson. Speed gave him power and made him feel as mighty as Joe Louis. He had his long arms wrapped about the steering wheel and his big foot jammed on the gas, thinking of how he could drive that goddam DeSoto taxicab straight off the mother-raping earth.

Margie lived in a flat on Franklin Avenue. It was a thirty-minute trip by rights, but the black boy made it in eighteen, Jackson biting his nails all the way.

Margie's husband hadn't come home from work. She looked like Imabelle, only more proper. She was straightening her hair when Jackson arrived and had a mean yellow look at being disturbed. The house smelled like a singed pig.

"Is Imabelle here?" Jackson asked, wiping the sweat from his head and face and pulling down the crotch of his pants.

"No, she is not. Why did not you telephone?"

"I didn't know y'all had a telephone. When'd y'all get it?"

17

"Yesterday."

"I ain't seen you since yesterday."

"No, you have not, have you?"

She went back to the kitchen where her hair irons were on the fire. Jackson followed her, keeping his overcoat on.

"You know where she might be?"

"Do I know where who might be?"

"Imabelle?"

"Oh, her? How do I know if you do not know? You are the one who is keeping her."

"Know where I can find Jodie, then?"

"Jodie? And who might Jodie be?"

"I don't know his last name. He's the man who told you and Imabelle about the man who raises money."

"Raises money for what?"

Jackson was getting mad. "Raises it to spend, that's for what. He raises dollar-bills into ten-dollar bills and ten-dollar bills into hundred-dollar bills."

She turned around from the stove and looked at Jackson.

"Is you drunk? If you is, I want you to get out of here and do not come back until you is sober."

"I ain't drunk. You sound more drunk than me. She met the man right here in your house."

"In my house? A man who raises ten-dollar bills into hundred-dollar bills? If you are not drunk, you is crazy. If I had met that man, he would still be here, chained to the floor, working his ass off every day."

"I ain't in no mood for joking."

"Do you think I am joking?"

"I mean the other one—Jodie. The one who knew the man who raises the money."

Margie picked up the straightening iron and began to run it through her kinky reddish hair. Smoke rose from the frying locks and a sound was heard like chops sizzling.

"God damn it, you have done made me burn my hair!" she raved.

"I'm sorry, but this is important."

"You mean my hair ain't important?"

18

"No, I don't mean that. I mean I got to find her."

She brandished the hot hair-iron like a club.

"Jackson, will you please take your ass away from here and let me alone? If Ima told you she met somebody in my house called Jodie, she is just lying. And if you do not know by this time that she is a lying bitch, you is a fool."

"That ain't no way to talk about your sister. I don't thank you for that one little bit."

"Who asked you to come here bothering me, anyway?" she shouted.

Jackson put on his hat and left in a huff. He began to feel cornered and panicky. He had to get his money raised before morning or he was jailhouse-bound. And he didn't know where else to look for Imabelle. He had met her at the Undertaker's Annual Dance in the Savoy Ballroom the year before. She'd been doing day work for the white folks downtown and didn't have a steady boyfriend. He'd started taking her out, but that had gotten to be so expensive she'd started living with him.

They didn't have any close friends. There was nowhere she could hide. She didn't like to get chummy with folks and didn't want anybody to know too much about her. He hardly knew anything about her himself. Just that she'd come from the South somewhere.

But he'd bet his life that she was true to him. Only she was scared of something and he didn't know what. That was what had him worried. She might have gotten so scared of the marshal she'd disappear for two or three days. He could telephone her white folks the next day to see if she'd shown up for work. But that would be too late. He needed her right then to get in touch with Hank to have his money raised, or they were both going to be in trouble.

He stopped in a drugstore and telephoned his landlady. But he put his handkerchief over the mouthpiece to disguise his voice.

"Is Imabelle Jackson there, ma'am?"

"I know who you is, Jackson. You ain't fooling me," his landlady yelled into the phone.

"Ain't nobody trying to fool you lady. I just asked you if Imabelle Jackson was there."

"No she ain't, Jackson, and if she was here she'd be in jail by now where you is going to be as soon as the police get hold of you. Busting up my brand-new stove and messing up my house and stealing money from your boss put aside to bury the dead, and the Lawd knows what else, trying to make out like you is somebody else when you telephone here, figuring I ain't gonna know your voice much as I done heard it asking me to leave you pay me the next week. Bringing that yallah woman into my house and breaking it up, good as I done been to you."

"I ain't trying to hide my voice. I'm just in a little trouble, that's all."

"You tellin' me! You is in more trouble than you knows."

"I'm going to pay you for the stove."

"If you don't I'm goin' to put you underneath the jail."

"You don't have to worry about that. I'm going to pay you first thing tomorrow."

"I go to work tomorrow."

"I'll pay you first thing when you come home from work."

"If you ain't in jail by then. What'd you steal from Mr. Clay?"

"I ain't stole nothing from nobody. What I wanted to ask was if Imabelle comes home you tell her to get in touch with Hank—"

"If she come here tonight, her or you either, and don't bring a hundred and fifty-seven dollars and ninety-five cents to pay for my stove, she ain't goin' to have no chance to get in touch with nobody, unless it be the judge she goin' to meet tomorrow morning."

"You call yourself a Christian," Jackson said angrily. "Here we are in trouble and—"

"Who's any worse Christian than you!" she shouted. "A thief and a liar! Living in sin! Busting my stove! Robbin' the dead! The Lawd don't even know you, I tell you that!"

20

She banged down the receiver so hard it stung Jackson's ears.

He left the booth, wiping the sweat from his round, shiny black face and head.

"Calls herself a Christian," he muttered to himself. "Couldn't be more of a devil if she had two horns."

He stood on the corner bareheaded, cooling his brain. There was nothing left now but to pray. He hailed a taxi, rode back to his minister's house on 139th Street in Sugar Hill.

Reverend Gaines was a big black man with a mighty voice, deeply religious. He believed in a fire-and-brimstone hell and had no sympathy for sinners whom he couldn't convert. If they didn't want to reform, accept the Lord, join the church, and live righteously, then burn them in hell. No two ways about it. A man couldn't be a Christian on Sunday and sin six days a week. Such a man must take God for a fool.

He was writing his sermon when Jackson arrived. But he put it aside for a good church-member.

"Welcome, Brother Jackson. What brings you to the house of the shepherd of the Lord?"

"I'm in trouble, Reverend."

Reverend Gaines fingered the satin lapel of his blue flannel smoking-jacket. The diamond on his third finger sparkled in the light.

"Woman?" he asked softly.

"No, sir. My woman's true. We're going to get married as soon as she gets her divorce."

"Don't wait too long, Brother. Adultery is a mortal sin."

"We can't do anything until she finds her husband."

"Money?"

"Yes, sir."

"Have you stolen some money, Brother Jackson?"

"Not exactly. I just need some money bad. Or it's going to look as if I stole some."

"Ah, yes, I understand," Reverend Gaines said. "Let us pray, Jackson."

21

"Yes, sir, that's what I want."

They knelt side by side on the carpeted floor. Reverend Gaines did the praying.

"Lord, help this brother to overcome his difficulties."

"Amen," Jackson said.

"Help him to get the money he needs by honest means."

"Amen."

"Help his woman find her husband so she can get her divorce and live righteously."

"Amen."

"Bless all the poor sinners in Harlem who find themselves having these many difficulties with women and money."

"Amen."

Reverend Gaines's housekeeper knocked at the door and stuck her head inside.

"Dinner is ready, Reverend," she said. "Mrs. Gaines has already sat down."

Reverend Gaines said, "Amen."

All Jackson could do was echo, "Amen."

"The Lord helps those who help themselves, Brother Jackson," Reverend Gaines said, hurrying off to dinner.

Jackson felt a lot better. His panic had passed and he began thinking with his head instead of his feet. The main thing was to have the Lord on his side. He had begun to think the Lord had quit him.

He caught a taxi on Seventh Avenue, rode down to 125th Street and turned over to the Last Word, a shoe-shine parlor and record shop at the corner of Eighth Avenue.

He put ninety dollars on numbers in the night house, playing five dollars on each. He played the *money row, lucky lady, happy days, true love, sun gonna shine, gold, silver, diamonds, dollars* and *whiskey*. Then to be on the safe side he also played *jail house, death row, lady come back, two-timing woman, pile of rocks, dark days* and *trouble*. He wasn't taking any chances.

While he was putting in his numbers behind blown-up pictures of Bach and Beethoven, the girl selling the real stuff played rock-and-roll records on request, and the shoe-shine boys were beating out the rhythm with their shine cloths. Jackson's feet took out with the beat, cutting out the steps, as though they didn't know about the trouble in his head.

Suddenly Jackson began feeling lucky. He gave up on the hope of finding Hank. He stopped worrying about Imabelle. He felt as though he could throw four fours in a row.

"Man, you know one thing, I feel good," he said to the shoe-shine boy.

"A good feeling is a sign of death, Daddy-o," the boy said.

Jackson put his faith in the Lord and headed for the dice game upstairs on 126th Street, around the corner.

CHAPTER 3

JACKSON climbed three flights of stairs and rapped on a red door in a brightly lit hall.

A metal disk moved from a round peephole. Jackson couldn't see the face, but the lookout saw him.

The door opened. Jackson went into an ordinary kitchen.

"You want to roll 'em or roll with 'em?" the lookout asked.

"Roll 'em," Jackson said.

The lookout searched him, took his fingernail knife and put it on the pantry shelf alongside several man-killing knives and hard-shooting pistols.

"How can I hurt anybody with that?" Jackson protested.

"You can jab out their eyes."

"The blade ain't long enough to go through the eyelid."

"Don't argue, man, just go down to the last door to the right," the lookout said, leaning against the door frame.

There were three loose nails in the door casing. By pressing them the lookout could blink the lights in the parlor, bedrooms, and dice room. One blink for a new customer, two for the law.

Another lookout opened the door from the inside of the dice room, closed and locked it behind Jackson.

There was a billiard table in the center of the room, and a rack holding billiard balls and cue sticks on one wall. The shooters were jammed about the table beneath a glare of light from a green-shaded drop lamp. The stick man stood on one side of the table, handling the dice and bets. Across from him sat the rack man on a high stool, changing greenbacks into silver dollars and banking the cuts. He

24

cut a quarter on all bets up to five dollars, and fifty cents on bets over five dollars.

The bookies sat at each end of the table. A squat, bald-headed, brown-skinned man called Stack of Dollars sat at one end; a gray-haired white man called Abie the Jew sat at the other. Stack of Dollars bet the dice to lose; took any bet to win. Abie the Jew bet the dice to win or lose, barring box cars and snake eyes.

It was the biggest standing crap game in Harlem.

Jackson knew all the famous shooters by sight. They were celebrities in Harlem. Red Horse, Four-Four and Coots were professional gamblers; Sweet Wine, Rock Candy, Chink and Beauty were pimps; Doc Henderson was a dentist; Mister Foot was a numbers banker.

Red Horse was shooting. He shook the number eight bird's-eye dice loosely in his left hand, rolled them with his right hand. The dice rolled evenly down the green velvet cover, jumped the dog chain stretched across the middle of the table like two steeplechasers in a dead heat, came to a stop on four and three.

"Four-trey, the country way," the stick man sang, raking in the dice. "Seven! The loser!"

Rock Candy reached for the money in the pot. Stack of Dollars raked in his bets. Abie took some, paid some.

"You goin' to buck 'em?" the stick man asked.

Red Horse shook his head. He could pay a dollar for three more rolls.

"Next good shooter," the stick man sang and looked at Jackson. "What you shoot, short-black-and-fat?"

"Ten bucks."

Jackson threw a ten-dollar bill and fifty cents into the circle. Red Horse covered it. The bettors got down, win and lose, in the books. The stick man threw the dice to Jackson, who caught the dice, held them in his cupped hand close to his mouth and talked to them.

"Just get me out of this trouble and I ain't goin' to ask for no more." He crossed himself, then shook the dice to get them hot.

"Turn 'em loose, Reverend," the stick man said. "They

25

ain't titties and you ain't no baby. Let 'em run wild in the big corral."

Jackson turned them loose. They hopped across the green like scared jackrabbits, jumped the dog chain like frisky kangaroos, romped toward Abie's field-cloth like locoed steers, got tired and rested on six and five.

"Natural eleven!" the stick man sang. "Eleven from heaven. The winner!"

Jackson let his money ride, threw another natural for the twenty; then crapped out for the forty with snake-eyes. He shot ten again, threw seven, let the twenty ride, threw another seven, shot the forty, and crapped out again. He was twenty dollars loser. He wiped the sweat from his face and head, took off his overcoat, put it with his hat on the coat rack, loosened the double-breasted jacket of his black hard-finished suit, and said to the dice, "Dice, I beg you with tears in my eyes as big as watermelons."

He shot ten again, crapped three times in a row, and asked the stick man to change the dice.

"These don't know me," he said.

The stick man put in some black-eyed number eight dice that were stone cold. Jackson warmed them in his crotch, and threw four naturals in a row. He had eighty dollars in the pot. He took down the fifty dollars he had lost and shot the thirty. He caught a four and jumped it, took down another fifty, and shot ten.

"Jealous man can't gamble, scared man can't win," the stick man crooned.

The bettors got off Jackson to win and bet him to lose. He caught six and sevened out.

"Shooter for the game," the stick man sang. "The more you put down the more you pick up."

The dice went on to the next shooter.

By midnight Jackson was $180 ahead. He had $376, but he needed $657.95 to cover the $500 he had stolen from Mr. Clay and the $157.95 to pay for his landlady's stove.

He quit and went back to the Last Word to see if he had hit on the numbers. The last word for that night was 919, dead man's row.

26

So Jackson went back to the dice game.

He prayed to the dice; he begged them. "I got pains in my heart as sharp as razor blades, and misery in my mind as deep as the bottom of the ocean and tall as the Rocky Mountains."

He took off his coat when it came his second turn to shoot. His shirt was wet. His trousers chafed his crotch. He loosened his suspenders when his third turn came and let them hang down his legs.

Jackson threw more natural sevens and elevens than had ever been seen in that game before. But he threw more craps, twos, threes and twelves, than he did natural sevens and elevens. And as all good crapshooters know, crapping is the way you lose.

Day was breaking when the game gave out. They had Jackson. He was stone-cold broke. He borrowed fifty cents from the house and trudged slowly down to the snack bar in the Theresa Hotel. He got a cup of coffee and two doughnuts for thirty cents and stood at the counter.

His eyes were glazed. His black skin had turned putty-gray. He was as tired as though he'd been plowing rocks with a mule team.

"You look beat," the counterman said.

"I feel low enough to be buried in whalebones, and they're on the bottom of the sea," he confessed.

The counterman watched him gobble his doughnuts and gulp his coffee.

"You must have got broke in that crap game."

"I did," Jackson confessed.

"Looks like it. They say a rich man can't sleep, but a broke man can't get enough to eat."

Jackson looked up at the clock on the wall and the clock said hurry-hurry. Mr. Clay came down from his living quarters at nine o'clock sharp. Jackson knew he'd have to be there with the money and find some way to slip it back into the safe when Mr. Clay opened it if he expected to get away with it.

Imabelle could raise the money, but he hated to ask her. It meant she'd have to be dishonest. But the kind of

27

trouble they were in now would make a rat eat red pepper.

He went into the hotel lobby next door and telephoned his apartment.

The Theresa lobby was dead at that hour save for a few working-johns who had to make eight o'clock time downtown, and were hurrying into the hotel grill for their morning grits and bacon.

His landlady answered.

"Is Imabelle come home?" he asked.

"Your yallah woman is in jail where you ought to be too," she answered evilly.

"In jail? How come?"

"Right after you phoned here last night a United States marshal brought her back here under arrest. He was looking for you too, Jackson, and if I'd knowed where you was I'd have told him. He wanted you both on a counterfeiting charge."

"A United States marshal? He had her under arrest? What'd he look like?"

"He said you knew him."

"What did he do with Imabelle?"

"He took her to jail, that's what. And he confiscated her trunk and took that along in case he didn't find you."

"Her trunk?" Jackson was so stunned he could barely speak. "He confiscated her trunk? And took it with him?"

"He sure did, lover boy. And when he finds you—"

"Good God! He confiscated her trunk? What did he say his name was?"

"Don't ask me no more questions, Jackson. I ain't going to get myself in any trouble helping you to escape."

"You ain't got a Christian bone inside of you," he said, and slowly hung up the receiver.

He stood sagging against the wall of the telephone booth. He felt as though he had stumbled into quicksand. Every time he struggled to get out, he went in deeper.

He couldn't figure out how the marshal managed to get hold of Imabelle's trunk. How had he found out what was

28

in it—unless he had scared her enough to make her tell? And that meant she was in trouble.

What made it so bad for Jackson was he didn't know where to look for the marshal. He had no idea where the marshal had taken Imabelle. He didn't believe the marshal had taken her to the federal jail because the marshal was out for all he could get. The marshal wouldn't take her trunk down to the jail if he expected to get a cut for himself. But Jackson had no idea how to go about tracing him. And he didn't know what he could do to save her trunk if he found the marshal.

He stood on the empty sidewalk in front of the Theresa, trying to think of a way out. His face was knotted from mental effort. Finally he muttered to himself, "There ain't no help for it."

He'd have to see his twin brother Goldy. Goldy knew everybody in Harlem.

He didn't know where Goldy lived, so he'd have to wait until noon when Goldy appeared on the street. He was afraid to loiter on the street himself. He didn't have the price of a movie, although there was one in the block that opened at eight o'clock in the morning. But there was a professional building around the corner on 125th Street with a number of doctors' offices.

He went up on the second floor and sat in a doctor's waiting room. The doctor hadn't arrived, but there were already four patients waiting. He kept moving back in line, after the doctor had arrived, letting everybody go ahead of him.

The receptionist kept looking at him from time to time. Finally she asked in a hard voice, "Are you sick or aren't you?"

By then it was almost noon.

"I was, but I feel better now," he said and put his hat on and left.

CHAPTER 4

THE PLATE-GLASS front of Blumstein's Department Store, exhibiting eye-catching items of wearing apparel and house furnishings for the residents of Harlem, extended from the back of the Theresa Hotel a half block down 125th Street.

A Sister of Mercy sat on a campstool to one side of the entrance, shaking a round black collection-box at the passersby and smiling sadly.

She was dressed in a long black gown, similar to the vestments of a nun, with a white starched bonnet atop a fringe of gray hair. A large gold cross, attached to a black ribbon, hung at her breast. She had a smooth-skinned, round black cherubic face, and two gold teeth in front which gleamed when she smiled.

No one paid her any special attention. There were many black Sisters of Mercy seen throughout Manhattan. They solicited in the big department-stores downtown, on Fifth Avenue, in the railroad stations, up and down 42nd Street and throughout Times Square. Only a few persons knew the name of the organization they belonged to. Most of the Harlem folk thought they were nuns, just the same as there were black, kinky-headed, frizzly-bearded rabbis seen about the streets.

She glanced up at Jackson and whispered in a prayerful voice, "Give to the Lawd, Brother. Give to the poor."

Jackson stopped to one side of her stool and examined the nylon stockings on display in the window.

A colored drunk staggering past, turned around and leered at the Sister of Mercy.

"Bless me, Sistah. Bless old Mose," he mumbled, trying to be funny.

" 'Knowest not that thou art wretched, and miserable, and poor, and blind, and naked,' sayeth the Lawd," the Sister quoted.

The drunk blinked and staggered hurriedly away.

A little black girl with witch-plaited hair ran up to the nun and said in a breathless voice, "Sistah Gabriel, Mama wants two tickets to heaven. Uncle Pone's dyin'."

She stuck two one-dollar bills into the nun's hand.

" 'Buy of me gold tried in the fire,' sayeth the Lawd," the nun whispered, tucking the bucks inside her gown. "What do she want two for, child?"

"Mama say Uncle Pone need two."

The nun slipped a black hand into the folds of her gown, drew out two white cards, and gave them to the little girl. Printed on the cards were the words:

ADMIT ONE
Sister Gabriel

"These'll take Uncle Pone to the bosom of the Lawd," she promised. " 'And I saw heaven opened, and beheld a white horse.' "

"Amen," the little girl said, and ran off with the two tickets to heaven.

"Shame on you, Goldy. Blaspheming the Lord like that," Jackson whispered. "The police are going to get you for selling those tickets."

"Ain't no law against it," Goldy whispered in reply. "They just say 'Admit One.' They don't say to where. Might be to the Savoy Ballroom."

"There's a law against impersonating a female," Jackson said disgustedly.

"You let the police take care of the law, Bruzz."

A couple approached to enter the store. Goldy rattled his coin box.

"Give to the Lawd, give to the poor," he begged prayerfully.

The woman stopped and dropped three pennies into the box.

Goldy's saintly smile went sour.

"Bless you, Mother, bless you. If three little pennies is all the Lawd is worth to you, then bless you."

The woman's dark brown skin turned purple. She dug up a dime.

"Bless you, Mother. Praise be the Lawd," Goldy whispered indifferently.

The woman went inside the store, but she could feel the eyes of the Lord pinned on her and the angels in heaven whispering among themselves, "What a cheapskate!" She was too ashamed to buy the dress she'd come for and she was unhappy all the rest of the day.

"I got to see you, Goldy," Jackson said, looking at the nylons in the window.

Two teen-age girls were passing at the time and heard him. They had no idea he was speaking to the Sister of Mercy and there was no one else nearby. They began giggling.

"A stockin' freak," one said.

The other replied, "He calls them Goldy, too."

Goldy brushed imaginary dust from his lap, took another look at Jackson's face, then stood up slowly, moving like an elderly woman, and folded the campstool.

"Stay in back of me," he whispered. " 'Way back."

He put the stool under one arm, jangled the coin box in the other hand, and trudged down the slushy sidewalk toward Seventh Avenue, blessing the colored folk who fed coins into the kitty. He looked like a tired, fat, saintly black woman, slaving in the service of the Lord.

He was a familiar sight. No one gave him a second look.

Seventh Avenue and 125th Street is the center of Harlem, the crossroads of Black America. On one corner was the largest hotel. Diagonally across from it was a big credit jewelry store with its windows filled with diamonds and watches selling for so much down and so much weekly. Next door was a book store with a big red-and-yellow sign reading: *Books Of 6,000,000 Colored People*. On the other corner was a mission church.

The people of Harlem take their religion seriously. If Goldy had taken off in a flaming chariot and galloped straight to heaven, they would have believed it—the godly and the sinners alike.

Goldy turned south on Seventh Avenue, past the Theresa Hotel entrance, past Sugar Rays Tavern, past the barber shop where the sharp cats got their nappy kinks straightened with a mixture of Vaseline and potash lye. He turned east on 121st Street into the Valley, climbed over piles of frozen garbage, kicked a mangy cur in the ribs, and entered a grimy tobacco-store which fronted for a numbers drop and reefer shop. Three teen-age boys had a fifteen-year-old girl inside, all blowing gage. They were trying to get her to undress.

"Go ahead, take 'em off, baby, take 'em off."

"Ain't nobody comin'. Go ahead and strip."

"Why don't you punks leave the girl alone," the proprietor said half-heartedly. "You can see she's 'shamed of her shape."

"I ain't 'shamed, neither," she said. "I got a good shape and I know it."

"Course you have," the proprietor said, winking at her lecherously.

He was a tall, dirty-looking yellow man with a lumpy pockmarked face and swimming red eyes.

"Bless the Lawd, Soldier," Goldy greeted him on entering. "Bless the Lawd, children." He gave the teen-agers a confidential look and quoted, " 'By these three was the third part of men killed, by the fire and by the smoke and by the brimstone which issued out of their mouths.' "

"Amen, Sister," the owner said, winking at Goldy.

The girl snickered. The boys fidgeted indecisively and shut up for a moment.

No one who noticed it thought it strange for a Sister of Mercy to kick a cur dog in the ribs, enter a dope den, and quote enigmatic Scripture to reefer-smoking delinquents.

33

In silence, Goldy waited for Jackson to catch up, then took him through the rear door, down a damp dark hallway, stinking of many varieties of excrement, and opened a padlocked door. He switched on a dim, fly-specked drop-lamp, slipped warily into a damp, cold, windowless room furnished with a scarred wooden table, two wobbly straight-backed chairs, a couch covered with dirty gray blankets. Against one wall, mildewed cardboard cartons were stacked one atop the other. The other dark-gray concrete walls sweated from the chill, damp air.

After Jackson had entered, Goldy padlocked the door on the inside and lit a rusty black kerosene stove which smoked and stank. He then threw the stool onto the couch, put his money box on the table, and sat down with a long sigh. He took off his white bonnet and gray wig.

Seen without his disguise, he was the spitting image of Jackson. White people in the South, where they had come from, had called them the Gold Dust Twins because of their resemblance to the twins pictured on the yellow boxes of Gold Dust soap powder.

"I don't live here," Goldy said. "This is just my office."

"I don't see how nobody could," Jackson said as he eased his weight onto one of the wobbly chairs.

"There's people lives in worse places," Goldy said.

Jackson wouldn't argue the point. "Goldy, there's something I want to ask you."

"I got to feed my monkey first."

Jackson looked about for the monkey.

"He's on my back," Goldy explained.

Jackson watched him with silent disgust as Goldy took an alcohol lamp, teaspoon and a hypodermic needle from the table drawer. Goldy shook two small papers of crystal cocaine and morphine into the spoon and cooked a C and M speedball over the flame. He groaned as he banged himself in the arm while the mixture was still warm.

"It's the same stuff as Saint John the Divine used," Goldy said. "Did you know that, Bruzz? You're a church-going man."

Jackson was glad none of his acquaintances knew he had

34

such a brother as Goldy, a dope-fiend crook impersonating a Sister of Mercy. Especially Imabelle. That'd be reason enough for her to quit him.

"I ain't never going to own you as my brother," he said.

"Well, Bruzz, that goes for me too. Now what's on your mind?"

"What I wanted to ask is do you know a colored United States marshal here in Harlem? He's a tall, slim colored man, and he's crooked too."

Goldy's ears perked up. "A colored U.S. marshal? And crooked? What you mean by crooked?"

"He's always trying to get bribes out of people."

Goldy smiled evilly. "What's the matter, Bruzz? You get shook down by some colored marshal?"

"Well, it was like this. I was having some money raised—"

"Raised?" Goldy's eyes popped.

"I was having ten-dollar bills raised into hundred-dollar bills."

"How much?"

"To tell the truth, all I had in the world. Fifteen hundred dollars."

"And you looked to get fifteen thousand?"

"Only twelve thousand, two hundred and fifty, after I paid off the commissions."

"And you got arrested?"

Jackson nodded. "During the operation the marshal broke into the kitchen and put us all under arrest. But the others got away."

Goldy burst out laughing and couldn't stop. The C and M speedball had taken hold and the pupils of his eyes had turned as black as ebony and had gotten as big as grapes. He laughed convulsively, as though he were having a fit. Tears streamed down his face. Finally he got himself under control.

"My own brother," he gasped. "Here us is, got the same mama and papa. Look just alike. And there you is, ain't got hep yet that you been beat. You has been swindled, man. You has been taken by The Blow. They take you for your money and they blow. You catch on? Changing tens into hundreds. What happened to your brains? You been drinking embalming fluid?"

Jackson looked more hurt than angry. "But I saw him do it once before," he said. "With my own eyes. I was looking right at him all the time. A man has got to believe his own eyes, ain't he?"

It hadn't been too hard for him to believe. Other people in Harlem believed that Father Divine was God.

"Sure, you saw him do it when he was sucking you in," Goldy said. "But what you didn't see was when he made the switch. That was when he turned to put the money into the stove to cook. What he put into the oven were just plain dummies along with a black-powder bomb. He put your money into a special pocket in the front of his coat."

"Then Imabelle got fooled, too. She was watching him, just the same as me. Neither of us saw him make the switch."

Goldy's eyelids drooped. "Who's Imabelle? Your old lady?"

"She's my woman. And she believed it even more than I did. It was her who first talked to Jodie, the man who told her about Hank. And Jodie looked like an honest, hard-working man, too."

It didn't surprise Goldy that Jackson had been trimmed on The Blow. Many smart men, even other con-men, had been stung by The Blow. There was something about raising the denomination of money that appealed to the larceny in men. But with women it was different. They were always suspicious of anything that was scientific. But he didn't know how Jackson felt about his woman, so all he said was,

"She's a trusting girl, she believe all that."

Jackson puffed up with indignation. "Do you think she'd let them cheat me if she didn't believe it, too?"

"What'd she do when the stove blew up? She try to help you save your money?"

"She tried all she could. But she ain't no Annie Oakley, carrying around two pistols. When that marshal bust into the kitchen waving his gun and flashing his badge, she ran like all the rest of us were trying to do. I was trying to run, too."

"They always catch the sucker. How else are they gonna blow with their sting? And you gave the marshal some more money to let you off?"

"I didn't know he was a crook. I gave him two hundred dollars."

"Where'd you get two hundred dollars, if he'd already taken all the money you had?"

"I had to take five hundred from Mr. Clay's safe."

Goldy whistled softly. "You give me the three hundred you got left, Bruzz, and I'll find those crooks and get all your money back."

"I haven't got it," Jackson confessed. "I lost it playing the numbers and shooting dice trying to get even."

Goldy pulled up the hem of his skirt and studied his fat black legs encased in black cotton stockings.

"For a man what calls himself a Christian, you've had yourself a night. Now what you goin' to do?"

"I got to find that man who posed as the marshal. After he took my two hundred dollars he arrested Imabelle so he could shake her down, too."

"You mean he worked another bribe out of your old lady after he got yours?"

"I don't know exactly what happened. I haven't seen her since she ran out of the kitchen with the rest of them. All I know is that when I telephoned my landlady she said a United States marshal brought Imabelle back into the house and that she was under arrest. Then he confiscated her trunk and took her away somewhere. And she hasn't been back since. That's what's got me so worried."

Goldy gave his brother an incredulous look. "Did you say he took her trunk?"

Jackson nodded. "She's got a big steamer-trunk."

Goldy stared so long at Jackson his eyes seemed fixed.

"What has she got in her trunk?"

Jackson evaded Goldy's stare. "Nothing but clothes and things."

37

Goldy kept staring at his brother.

Finally he said, "Bruzz, listen to me close. If all that broad has got in her trunk is clothes, she has teamed up with that slim stud and helped him to swindle you. How long is it goin' to take you to see that?"

"She ain't done that," Jackson contradicted flatly. "She got no need to. I'd have given her all the money if she'd asked for it."

"How you know she ain't sweet on the stud? Might not be your money she's after. Might just be a change of sheets."

Jackson's wet-black face became swollen with anger.

"Don't talk like that about her," he said threateningly. "She ain't sweet on nobody but me. We're going to get married. Besides, she ain't seen nobody else."

Goldy shrugged. "You figure it out yourself then, Bruzz. She's gone off with the man who beat you out o' your money. If she don't want the man and if she don't want the money—"

"She ain't run off, he taken her off," Jackson interrupted. "Besides which, if she'd wanted money she got her own money, herself. She can put her hand on more money than either you or me have ever seen."

Goldy's fat black body went dead still. Not an eyelash flickered, not a muscle moved in his face. He seemed not to breathe. If she had more money than either of them had ever seen, it was getting down to the nitty-gritty. Those were facts he understood. Money! And she had it stashed in her trunk, else why did she and the slim stud come back for it? She couldn't have had any clothes in there worth taking, not after living with a low-paid flunky like his twin brother.

His huge black-pupiled eyes lingered trance-like on Jackson's wet, worried face.

"I'm goin' to help you find your gal, Bruzz," he whispered confidentially. "After all, you is my twin brother."

He took a small bottle from his gown and handed it to Jackson. "Have a little taste."

Jackson shook his head.

"Go ahead and take a taste," Goldy urged irritably. "If the devil ain't already got your soul after all you done last night, you is saved. Take a good taste. We're going out and look for that stud and your gal, and you is goin' to need all the courage you can get."

Jackson wiped the mouth of the bottle with his dirty handkerchief and took a deep drink. The next instant he was gasping for breath. It had tasted like musty tequila flavored with chicken bile, and it had burned his gullet like cayenne pepper.

"Lord in Heaven!" he gasped. "What's that stuff?"

"Ain't nothing but smoke," Goldy said. "There's lots of folks here in the Valley won't drink nothing else."

The drink numbed Jackson's brain. He forgot what he'd come there for. He sat on the couch trying to get his thoughts together.

Goldy sat across the table, silently staring at him. Goldy's huge, black-pupiled eyes were hypnotic. They looked like glinting black pools of evil. Jackson tried to tear his gaze away but couldn't.

Finally Goldy stood up and put on his wig and bonnet. He hadn't said anything yet.

Jackson tried to stand too, but the room began to spin. He suddenly suspected Goldy of poisoning him.

"I'll kill you," he said thickly, trying to spring toward his brother.

But the walls of the little room were spinning like a million buzz saws rotating about his head. He couldn't defend himself when Goldy took him beneath the armpits and laid him on the couch.

CHAPTER 5

GOLDY lived with two other men on the Golden Ridge of Convent Avenue, north of City College and 140th Street. They had the ground floor of a brownstone private house that had been cut up into apartments.

All three impersonated females and lived by their wits. All were fat and black, which made it easy.

The biggest one, known as Big Kathy, was the land-prop of a house of prostitution in the Valley, on 131st Street east of Seventh Avenue. His house was known far and wide as The Circus.

The other had a flat on 116th Street where he worked the fortune-telling pitch, billing himself as Lady Gypsy. There was a card on his door that read:

> LADY GYPSY
> Fortune Telling
> Prognostications
> Formulations
> Interpretations
> Revelations
> Numbers Given

An old woman known as Mother Goose cleaned and cooked for them. At home they always acted with decorum. All of them were on junk, but they never used it in their house. They never entertained. At night a shaded floor-lamp shone in the front window, but no one was ever seen. That was because no one was ever there. They had the reputation of being the most respectable women on a street where the colored folk were so respectable they'd phone the sanitation department to remove cat droppings from the sidewalk. People in the neighborhood knew them as the Three Black Widows.

Goldy had a wife who lived in a flat in Lenox Avenue next door to the Savoy Ballroom. But she worked in domestic service for a white family in White Plains, and was home only on Thursdays and every other Sunday afternoon. On those days Sister Gabriel was missing from his customary haunts.

When Goldy left Jackson he went home to have breakfast with Big Kathy and Lady Gypsy. They were having baked ham, lye hominy, stewed okra and corn, Southern biscuits, and finished with sweet-potato pie and muscatel wine. Mother Goose served them silently.

"How does it look outside?" Big Kathy asked Goldy.

"Cool and clear," Goldy said. "No one has been killed, carved up, robbed, or run over this morning, to my knowledge. But there's some new studs in town cooking with The Blow."

"That old hick-town pitch!" Lady Gypsy exclaimed. "Here in Harlem? Who're they going to get with that?"

"There's fools everywhere," Goldy said. "It's the Christians full of larceny who fall for that."

"Hush, man! Don't I know it?"

"Well, if they'd made a sting I'm sure I would have seen them," Big Kathy said.

"They made a sting all right," Goldy said. "Fifteen C's."

"That's strange," Big Kathy said. "They ain't been in my place yet to get their ashes hauled. They must be on the lam from somewhere."

"I hadn't thought of that angle," Goldy said.

Before leaving, Goldy telephoned Jackson's landlady.

"I'm the United States Federal Attorney, and I'd like some information about a couple who lived in your house by the name of Jackson and Imabelle Perkins."

"You mean you is the DA?" she asked in an awed tone.

"No, I'm the FA."

"Oh, you is the FA. Lawd Almighty, they's in big trouble, ain't they?" she said happily.

She told him everything she knew about them except where to find them.

41

But he got the name of Imabelle's sister and telephoned her next.

"This is Rufus," he said. "You don't know me but I'm a friend of Imabelle's husband back home."

"I didn't know she had a husband back home."

"Sure you know she's got a husband back home."

"If he's the same kind of husband she got here then she got two husbands."

"I don't want to argue about that. I just want to know if she's still got the stuff in her trunk."

"What stuff?"

"You know—*the* stuff."

"I do not know what stuff you are talking about, whoever you might be. And I do not know anything about my sister's husbands, wherever they might be," she said, and hung up.

Next Goldy telephoned Imabelle's white employers, but they said she hadn't been to work for three days.

So he put on his gray wig and white bonnet and went down to the Harlem branch post-office on 125th Street to study the rogue's gallery of wanted criminals.

There were pictures of three colored men wanted in Mississippi for murder. That meant they had killed a white man because killing a colored man wasn't considered murder in Mississippi. Goldy studied the faces a long time. No one looked twice at the black-gowned Sister of Mercy studying the faces of wanted criminals.

Instead of returning to his stand beside the entrance to Blumstein's Department Store, Goldy made a round of the bars and joints where they were most likely to hang out. He went up Seventh Avenue to 145th Street, east to Lenox Avenue, south on Lenox to 125th Street again. He jangled his coin box and murmured in his husky, prayerful voice, "Give to the Lord. Give to the poor." Whenever anyone looked at him suspiciously he quoted from *Revelation,* " 'That ye may eat the flesh of kings.' "

"If that's what you're goin' to buy with the money, Sister, here's a half a dollar," a colored woman said.

There were more bars on his itinerary than on any other comparable distance on earth. In every one the jukeboxes blared, honeysuckle-blues voices dripped stickily through jungle cries of wailing saxophones, screaming trumpets, and buckdancing piano-notes; someone was either fighting, or had just stopped fighting, or was just starting to fight, or drinking ruckus-juice and talking about fighting. Others were talking about numbers. "Man, I had twelve bones on two twenty-seven and two thirty-seven came out." Or talking about hits and misses. "Man, I saw that chick and hit. Man, I struck solid gold." Or talking about love. "That was when my love came down, sugar, and that was the bitter end."

He stopped in the dice games, the bookie joints, the barbecue stands, the barber shops, professional offices, undertakers', flea-heaven hotels, grocery stores, meat markets called "The Hog Maw," "Chitterling Country," "Pig Foot Heaven." He questioned dope pushers whom he could trust.

"Have you picked up on a new team, Jack?"

"Pitching what?"

"The Blow."

"Naw, Sister, that's for the sticks."

Some knew him as a man, others thought he was a hophead Sister. It didn't make any difference to them either way.

He looked at all the faces everywhere he went.

When the coins dropped lightly into his box, he gave out a number, quoting from *Revelation*, " 'Let him that hath understanding count the number of the beast . . . and his number is six hundred threescore and six.' " Jokers dropped quarters and half-dollars into his box and rushed to the nearest numbers drop to play six-six-six.

He was worn-out by the time he went home to eat supper. He hadn't got a lead.

Big Kathy and Lady Gypsy were at business. He ate alone and had Mother Goose give him what was left in the pot to take to Jackson.

CHAPTER 6

WHEN JACKSON woke up he found himself lying on the couch covered with the two dirty blankets. His joints were stiff as rigor mortis and his head ached like a jack hammer was drilling in his skull. The dim light burnt his eyes like pepper and his mouth was cotton-dry.

He twisted his neck as carefully as though it were made of glass. He saw Goldy sitting at the table in his sloppy black gown but minus his bonnet and wig. A covered pot sat before him on the table. Beside it were a loaf of sliced white bread in oiled-paper wrapping and a bottle half full of whiskey.

The air was blue with smoke and thick with kerosene fumes. The room was cold.

Goldy sat dreamily blowing on the gold cross he wore about his neck and shining it with a handkerchief gray from dirt.

Jackson threw off the blankets, staggered to his feet, grabbed Goldy's fat greasy neck between his two black hands, and began to squeeze. Sweat beaded on his black face like pox pimples. His eyes had turned fire-red and looked stark crazy.

Goldy's eyes popped and his face turned rusty gray. He dropped the cross, grabbed Jackson back of the neck with both hands, jerked down with all his strength, and butted heads with him. The momentum tipped his chair over backward and he went down on his back with Jackson on top of him, both knocked groggy by the butting. The bottle of whiskey fell to the floor without breaking, and rolled beneath the couch.

The blankets had sailed over the kerosene stove and were beginning to sizzle with the smell of burning wool and cotton.

The brothers threshed about the floor, grunting like two hungry cannibals fighting over the missing rib. Finally Goldy got his foot in Jackson's belly and gave a shove, separating them.

"What's the matter with you, man," he panted. "You done blown your top?"

"You doped me!" Jackson wheezed.

The blankets draped over the stove began to burn.

"Now look what you done," Goldy said, trying to free his left foot from the folds of his gown so he could get up.

Jackson clutched the edge of the table, knocking off the loaf of bread while clambering to his feet, then stepped on it as he lunged for the burning blankets. He snatched up the blankets to throw them outside, but the door was padlocked on the inside.

"Open the door," he coughed.

The room was black dark with smoke.

"You done made me lose the key," Goldy accused, scrabbling about the floor on his hands and knees looking for it.

"Goddammit, help me find the key," he shouted angrily.

Jackson threw the blankets to the floor, and began crawling about helping Goldy search for the key.

"What do you lock the door for all the time?" he complained.

"Here it is," Goldy said.

Getting to his feet to unlock the door he stepped on the bread also.

Jackson kicked the blankets into the hallway.

"You're going to be found dead locked up in here someday," he said.

"You ain't got the brains you were born with," Goldy said, pushing Jackson aside to get through to the store for water to throw onto the smoking blankets.

Afterwards he tore up a carton and gave Jackson a piece of cardboard to help fan the smoke from the room,

45

bellyaching the while, "Here I is, putting myself out to help you just because you is my brother, and there you is, trying to kill me first thing."

"How are you trying to help me," Jackson grumbled while he fanned the smoke. "I come to you for help and you give me a mickey finn."

"Aw, man, eat your dinner and shet up."

Jackson picked up the squashed loaf of bread and straightened it out, then sat at the table and lifted the lid of the pot. It was half-filled with boiled pig's feet, black-eyed peas and rice.

"Ain't nothin' but hoppin' john," Goldy said.

"I like hoppin' john, all right," Jackson replied.

Goldy closed the door and padlocked it again. Jackson gave him a disapproving look. Goldy found the bottle of whiskey beneath the couch and poured Jackson a slug. Jackson looked at it suspiciously. Goldy gave him an evil look.

"You wouldn't even trust our mama, would you?" he said, taking a swallow to show it wasn't doped.

Jackson took a drink and grimaced.

"Do you make this stuff yourself?"

"Man, quit beefing. You ain't givin' me no money to buy you no good whiskey, so drink that and shet up."

Jackson began to eat with an aggrieved expression. Goldy cooked a C and M speedball and banged himself with quiet savor.

"I called your landlady," he said finally. "Imabelle ain't come back."

Jackson stopped eating in the middle of a chew. "I got to go out and find her."

"Naw, you ain't, unless you want to get arrested by the first cop you run into. Your boss has got a warrant out for you."

Sweat started forming on Jackson's face. "That don't make no difference. She might be in trouble."

"She ain't in no trouble. You the one what's in trouble."

Jackson dropped a polished foot-bone atop the pile on the table, wiped his mouth with the back of his hand, and

46

looked at Goldy with the deadly indignation of a puritan.

"Listen, if you think I'm going to set here after being cheated out of my money and kidnapped out of my woman, you got another think coming. She's my woman. I'm going to look for her too."

"Take a drink and relax. You can't find her tonight. Let's give this business a little thought."

He poured Jackson another drink. Jackson looked at it with distaste then downed it with a gulp and gasped.

"What kind of thought?"

"That's what I want to know. Just what kind of things has your woman got in that trunk besides clothes?"

Jackson blinked. The food and the whiskey and the close air in the small tight room were making him sleepy.

"Heirlooms."

"Come again."

Jackson's thoughts were growing fuzzy and he suspected Goldy of trying to trick him.

"Copper pots and pans and bowls," he shouted angrily. "Stuff that was given to her when she got married."

"Copper pots! Pans and bowls!" Goldy looked at him incredulously. "You want me to believe that her and that slim man has gone off somewhere to cook?"

Jackson was so sleepy he could barely keep his eyes open.

"Just leave her trunk alone," he mumbled belligerently. "If you want to help, just help me find her, and leave her things alone."

"That's all I'm tryin' to do, Bruzz," Goldy protested. "Just tryin' to help you find your gal-friend. But I don't know yet what I'm looking for."

Jackson was too sleepy to reply. He stretched out on the couch and went to sleep instantly.

"The stuff was too strong," Goldy muttered to himself.

CHAPTER 7

BY KEEPING Jackson doped half the time and scared the other half, Goldy held him prisoner in the room. Every day he told Jackson he was working on a lead and promised him definite news by evening. But it was three days later before he got his first real lead.

The Three Black Widows were having breakfast when Big Kathy said, "There was a con man called Morgan in my place last night. He was big-mouthing to my girls about how he was going to make a fortune by the lost-gold-mine pitch. You think he's one of them you're looking for?"

Goldy became alert. "Could be. What kind of a stud was he?"

"The con-man type, half-sized and sharp but not flashy, a smooth money-talker but stingy, cat-eyed, about forty. And he looked dangerous."

"He is dangerous."

"He's one then?"

"The front man. How're they goin' to work it?"

"He didn't say. When Teena tried to dig him he clammed up and got his ashes hauled and beat it."

"Did she find out where they're making their pitch?"

"Naw, he acted as if he'd talked too much already."

"He'll be back," Goldy said philosophically.

"Yeah, that girl plays 'em for the long haul."

That evening after Jackson had finished the pot of pig's ears, collard greens and okra Goldy had taken him, and Goldy had had his evening bang, Goldy said casually, "I heard today there's a man just come to Harlem who's found a real lost gold-mine somewheres."

48

Suddenly Jackson began trembling and sweat popped from his head and face like showers of rain.

"A gold-mine?"

"That's what I said. A real lost gold-mine. And the word is out that they got a trunk full of gold ore to prove it." He peered at Jackson through narrowed eyes. "Does that mean anything to you, Bruzz?"

Jackson looked suddenly sick, as though he'd swallowed a live bullfrog and it was trying to hop back out of his throat. He wiped the sweat from his ashy face and looked at Goldy through sick eyes.

"Goldy, listen, that gold ore doesn't really belong to Imabelle. That's the only reason I haven't said anything about it. It belongs to her husband. She's got to give every ounce of it back whenever she gets her divorce or he'll send her to the penitentiary. She told me."

"So that's it, Bruzz." Goldy leaned back in his chair and regarded his brother with rapt contemplation. "So that's it. That's what she's got in her trunk. You've been holding out on me, Bruzz."

"I ain't been holding out. I just didn't want you to get no ideas because that gold ore don't belong to her. I wouldn't even touch an ounce of it myself, no matter how hard up I was."

"How much is it, Bruzz? Can't be all that much or you wouldn't be losin' all your money on The Blow trying to get it raised and then stealin' money from your boss."

"That ain't got nothing to do with it. It's just that it doesn't belong to her. Do you think I'd steal some of it for myself and risk her getting sent to the penitentiary?"

"Naw, I know you wouldn't do that, Bruzz. You is too honest. But just how much is it?"

"There's two hundred pounds and eleven ounces."

Goldy whistled and his eyes popped out like skinned bananas. "Two hundred pounds! Jumping Jesus! You've seen it, ain't you? You've really seen it?"

"Of course I've seen it. Lots of times. We used to take some of it out and put it on the table and sit there with the

49

door locked and look at it. She never tried to hide it from me."

Goldy sat staring at his brother as though he couldn't remove his gaze.

"What does it look like, Bruzz?"

"It looks like gold ore. What do you think it looks like?"

"Can you see the pure gold?"

"Sure you can see the pure gold. There're layers of gold running through the rocks."

"What kind of layers? Thin layers or thick layers?"

"Thick layers. What do you think? There's as much gold as there is rock."

"Then there's about a hundred pounds of pure gold, you'd say?"

"About that."

"A hundred pounds of pure gold." Goldy blew on his gold cross and began polishing it dreamily.

"Bruzz, listen to me. If that gold ore is the real stuff, solid eighteen-carat gold, your gal is in real trouble. If it ain't, then she's working with 'em and done helped them to trim you. Ain't no two ways about it."

"I've been telling you they're holding her prisoner. Been telling you all the time," Jackson said indignantly. "Do you think she'd be toting around a trunk full of gold ore if it wasn't real eighteen-carat solid gold?"

"I ain't thinking nothing. I'm asking you. Do you know for sure that gold ore is solid eighteen-carat?"

"I know for sure," Jackson stated solemnly. "It's real gold ore, as pure as it was dug out of the ground. That's why I'm so worried."

"That's all I want to know."

Goldy knew that his brother was a square, but he figured that even a five-cornered square ought to be able to tell pure gold that has come straight out of the ground.

"Do you know where I can get a pistol?" Jackson asked suddenly.

Goldy stiffened. "A pistol? What you goin' to do with a pistol?"

"I'm going out of here and get my woman and her gold ore. I ain't going to set here no longer and wait on you."

"Man, listen to me. Those studs is wanted in Mississippi for killing a white man. Those studs is dangerous. All you'd do with a pistol is get yourself killed. What good are you goin' to be to your woman when you is dead?"

"I'm not going to fight them fair," Jackson said wildly.

"Man, you has gone raving crazy. You don't even know where they is at."

"I'll find them if I have to search every hole in Harlem."

"Man, Saint Peter himself don't know where every hole is at in Harlem. I've seen grandpappy rats get so lost in these holes they find themselves shacked up with a sewer full of eels."

"Then I'll rob somebody and get some money and hire somebody to help me."

"Take it easy, Bruzz. I'm goin' to find them for you. Where is your religion at? Where is your faith? Your time's comin', man."

Jackson wiped his stinging red eyes with his dirty handkerchief.

"It'd better hurry up and come soon," he said.

CHAPTER 8

THEY WERE having a big ball in the Savoy and people were lined up for a block down Lenox Avenue, waiting to buy tickets. The famous Harlem detective-team of Coffin Ed Johnson and Grave Digger Jones had been assigned to keep order.

Both were tall, loose-jointed, sloppily dressed, ordinary-looking dark-brown colored men. But there was nothing ordinary about their pistols. They carried specially made long-barreled nickel-plated .38-calibre revolvers, and at the moment they had them in their hands.

Grave Digger stood on the right side of the front end of the line, at the entrance to the Savoy. Coffin Ed stood on the left side of the line, at the rear end. Grave Digger had his pistol aimed south, in a straight line down the sidewalk. On the other side, Coffin Ed had his pistol aimed north, in a straight line. There was space enough between the two imaginary lines for two persons to stand side by side. Whenever anyone moved out of line, Grave Digger would shout, "Straighten up!" and Coffin Ed would echo, "Count off!" If the offender didn't straighten up the line immediately, one of the detectives would shoot into the air. The couples in the queue would close together as though pressed between two concrete walls. Folks in Harlem believed that Grave Digger Jones and Coffin Ed Johnson would shoot a man stone dead for not standing straight in a line.

Grave Digger looked around and saw the black-gowned figure of Sister Gabriel trudging slowly down the street.

"What's the word, Sister?" he greeted.

" '*And I saw three unclean spirits like frogs come out of the mouth of the dragon,* the sixth angel said,' " Sister Gabriel quoted.

The couples nearby in the queue laughed.

"Listen to Sistah Gabriel," a young woman snickered.

"I hear you, Sister," Grave Digger said. "And what makes those three frogs hop?"

The listeners laughed again.

Sister Gabriel paused. " 'For they are the spirits of devils, working miracles.' "

"Do you think she's crazy?" a loud whisper was heard.

"Shut your mouth," came a cautious reply.

"And these frogs?" Grave Digger kept it up. "You mean they've got a frog pond in Harlem?"

It was a signal for the listeners to laugh again.

" 'And upon her forehead was a name written, Mystery,' " Sister Gabriel quoted and moved on.

"Everybody to their own Jesus," Grave Digger said to the audience.

Goldy continued down Lenox Avenue to 131st Street and turned the corner toward Big Kathy's whorehouse.

It was a six-room apartment on the second floor rear of a big crumbling five-story building. Big Kathy was giving her customers a show and the big living-room was lit brightly for the occasion. The air was tinted blue with the smoke of incense. Five girls and a dozen men sat squeezed together on shabby overstuffed chairs and sofas backed against the walls, leaving the center of the room clear.

A huge yellow woman, almost six feet tall and weighing almost two hundred and fifty pounds, was struggling furiously with a short, skinny, muscular black man about half her weight. Both were clad in skintight rubber suits that had been greased and their faces were streaming with sweat that couldn't escape through the body pores.

They were working off a bet whether he could throw her. The stake was a hundred dollars. Side bets had been made.

The big woman was clubbing the little man with her fists. The little man was trying to get hold of the big woman's greased limbs. It was rugged. The spectators were laughing and shouting obscene encouragement.

"Give him some more love licks, baby," a man kept shouting.

Goldy entered by the service door and went unnoticed down the hall to Big Kathy's private room. He entered without knocking.

The room was furnished with a bed, chiffonier, a desk for a dressing table, and two red plastic-covered chairs.

Big Kathy was standing at the foot of the bed beside a hinged panel that opened inward from the wall at the height of his face. When closed, the panel was hidden by a lithograph of Mary and her Child. On the other side was a transparent mirror giving a clear view of the living room without the peeper's being seen.

Big Kathy turned his head and beckoned to Goldy.

"He's here," he whispered. "Over by the radio with Teena in his lap."

Goldy put his face to the peephole and Big Kathy looked over his shoulder. He spotted Hank instantly. Then he noticed a rough-skinned, broad-shouldered man with half-straightened hair, dressed in working pants and a leather jacket, sitting beside Hank in a straight-backed chair.

"That's another one," Goldy whispered. "The one beside him with the burnt hair."

"He calls himself Walker."

Goldy's gaze roved about the room but he didn't see the slim man.

"Can you get Teena in here?" he asked Big Kathy.

Big Kathy fingered a loose nail in the joist on which the panel was hinged. The radio dial lit up. All five girls in the big room looked at it covertly.

Then Teena got up and excused herself.

"I've got to go wee-wee."

"You're getting kind of old for that, ain't you?" Jodie said roughly.

"Quit picking at her," Hank ordered.

Teena slipped into Big Kathy's room without its being noticed.

54

"The Sister here wants you to dig your John tonight about his gold-mine pitch, and to get every angle there is," Big Kathy said.

Teena looked at the Sister of Mercy curiously. She had discovered by accident that Big Kathy was a man, but she didn't know anything definite about Goldy.

"What's her story?" she asked impudently.

"You're drinking too much," Big Kathy said. "You'd better be sober when you get to work, and you'd better not miss."

"I ain't goin' to miss," Teena said sullenly.

As soon as she'd returned to the sitting room, Big Kathy went in and stopped the wrestling match.

"Let's call it a draw."

"Let 'em finish!" Jodie shouted. "I got my money up."

"Take it down then," Big Kathy said harshly. "I said it's a draw."

The wrestlers were on the point of exhaustion and glad to quit.

Jodie took down the money from the girl who was holding the bet and pushed his way toward the outside door. Big Kathy let him out.

Teena took Hank to a room.

Goldy stretched out on Big Kathy's bed, but he was too tense to sleep. He was too worried about whether the gold ore was real. He believed Jackson, but he wanted to be sure.

Big Kathy sat in one of the plastic-covered armchairs, skirt drawn up above his big lumpy knees, reading the society page of a Negro weekly newspaper and commenting from time to time about friends of his who were mentioned.

They had a long wait. It was after midnight before Teena knocked softly.

"Come in," Big Kathy said.

"Whew!" Teena whistled, flopping into the other chair. "He talked my ear off."

Goldy sat up on the edge of the bed and leaned forward. "Did he want you to go in with them?"

55

"Hell, no! That stingy son of a bitch! He was tryin' to sell me some shares."

"Then you struck," Big Kathy said.

"I got everything but where they're making the pitch."

Goldy looked disappointed. "That was one of the main things."

"I did my best, but he wouldn't give."

"All right," Big Kathy said. "Let's have what you got."

"It's just the old lost-gold-mine pitch. The one they call Walker is supposed to be the prospector who accidentally discovered the lost gold mine in Mexico. It's the biggest and richest gold mine he's ever seen in all his years of prospecting, and all that bullshit."

"Let's hear it anyhow," Goldy said.

Teena threw him another calculating look.

"Well, Walker's afraid he'd be killed if he even so much as mentioned finding the mine. And naturally the only man he can trust to tell about it is Mr. Morgan, who's a big-time financier from Los Angeles. Mr. Morgan's known all over the West Coast for backing big business-deals and has got a reputation from coast to coast for being honest."

She started giggling.

"Go on," Big Kathy said roughly.

"Well, what prospector Walker needed was thousands of dollars' worth of tools and equipment and stuff and about a hundred miners to work for him. And besides that he's got to get a permit from the Mexican government to work the mine, which is going to cost a hundred thousand dollars just by itself.

"So the first thing Mr. Morgan does is engage the services—that's what he said—engage the—"

"Get on with the story," Big Kathy said.

"Engage the services of a gold assayer from the Federal Bureau of Assayers. I ain't seen that one, but they call him Goldsmith."

She began giggling again but a look from Big Kathy stopped her.

"Well, all three of them, Walker and Morgan and Goldsmith, was supposed to have gone to Mexico to investigate the mine. But when Mr. Morgan found out how big it was he knew he couldn't swing the deal alone. There were billions of dollars' worth of gold in the mine and it'd take half a million dollars to mine it right. Morgan said he could have financed it through his bank—he told me this straight to my face—but he didn't want the white folks to get control of it and take all the profits. So he decided to organize a corporation and sell stock just to colored folks. They're going all over the whole United States selling stock at fifty dollars a share; and to give themselves time to make a load they're telling everybody it'll take six months to get the mine in operation and another three or four months before it starts paying off."

She stopped and lit a cigarette, then looked from one to the other. "Well, that's it."

"How're they selling their stock if you couldn't find out where they're making their pitch?" Goldy asked intently.

"Oh, I forgot to tell you about that. They got a contact man called Gus Parsons, or Gus somebody-or-other. He's working all the plush bars, attending businessmen's conferences, even going to church festivals, Morgan said, contacting the suckers. Investors, Morgan calls them. Then he takes them to their headquarters blindfolded, in his own car."

Big Kathy's eyes narrowed as he looked at Teena.

Goldy kept his intent stare pinned on her.

"How come all that?" he asked.

Teena shrugged. "He said they're afraid of being robbed."

"Robbed?" Big Kathy echoed.

"Robbed of what?" Goldy asked.

"He say they got a trunk full of gold ore, whatever that is. He said it was taken from the lost mine, as if anybody'd believe that shit."

"Do they keep it at their headquarters?" Goldy asked.

There was something in Goldy's voice that made Big Kathy look at him sharply.

Teena didn't know what was happening and she began getting scared.

"I don't know where they keep it. He didn't say nothing to me about that. All he said to me was they had samples at headquarters to exhibit but if anybody had enough money to invest, they'd show 'em a whole trunk full of pure gold ore."

Goldy sighed so softly it sounded as though he were crying to himself.

Big Kathy kept staring at him with his eyes full of questions. "You through with Teena?"

Goldy nodded.

"Get out," Big Kathy said.

As soon as Teena had closed the door, he leaned far over and stared into Goldy's bowed face.

"It is true?"

Goldy nodded slowly. "It's true."

"How much?"

"Enough for everybody."

"What do you want me to do?"

"Just play dead until after I have got it."

CHAPTER 9

GRAVE DIGGER and Coffin Ed weren't crooked detectives, but they were tough. They had to be tough to work in Harlem. Colored folks didn't respect colored cops. But they respected big shiny pistols and sudden death. It was said in Harlem that Coffin Ed's pistol would kill a rock and that Grave Digger's would bury it.

They took their tribute, like all real cops, from the established underworld catering to the essential needs of the people—gamekeepers, madams, streetwalkers, numbers writers, numbers bankers. But they were rough on purse snatchers, muggers, burglars, con men, and all strangers working any racket. And they didn't like rough stuff from anybody else but themselves. "Keep it cool," they warned. "Don't make graves."

When Goldy got to the Savoy they were just leaving with two studs who'd got into a knife fight about a girl. The stud who'd brought the girl had gotten jealous because she'd danced too much with another stud. What made Coffin Ed and Grave Digger mad was the girl had put these two studs to fighting so she could slip away with a third stud, and these two studs were too simple-minded to see it.

Goldy followed them to the 126th Street precinct station in a taxi.

The big booking-room where the desk sergeant sat behind a fortress-like desk five feet high on the side toward the detective bureau was jampacked with the night's pickup.

The patrol-car cops, foot patrolmen, plainclothes dicks all had their prisoners in tow, waiting to book them on the blotter at the desk. The desk sergeant was taking them in turn, writing down their names, charges, addresses, and arresting-officers on the blotter, before turning them over to the jailors who hung waiting in the background.

The small-time bondsmen, white and colored, were hanging about the desk and threading among the prisoners, soliciting business. For a ten-dollar fee they went bail for misdemeanors.

The cops were angry because they'd have to appear in court the next morning during their off-hours to testify against the prisoners they'd arrested. They were impatient to get their prisoners booked so they could go to some of their hangouts and take a nap before quitting time.

A young white cop had arrested a middle-aged drunken colored woman for prostitution. The big rough brown-skinned man dressed in overalls and a leather jacket picked up with her claimed she was his mother and he was just walking her home.

"Gettin' so a woman can't even walk down the street with her own natural-born son," the woman complained.

"Shut up, can't you?" the cop said irritably.

"Don't you tell my mama to shut up," the man said.

"If this whore's your mama, I'm Santa Claus," the cop said.

"Don't you call me no whore," the woman said, and slammed the cop in the face with her pocketbook.

The cop struck back instinctively and knocked the woman down. The colored man hit the cop above the ear and knocked him down. Another cop let go his own prisoner and sapped the man about the head. The man staggered head-forward into another cop, who slapped him again. In the excitement someone stepped on the woman and she began screaming.

"Help! Help! They's tramplin' me!"

"They's killin' a colored woman!" another prisoner yelled.

Everybody began fighting.

The desk sergeant looked down from the sanctuary of his desk and said in a bored voice, "Jesus Christ."

At that moment Coffin Ed and Grave Digger entered with their two prisoners.

"Straighten up!" Grave Digger shouted in a stentorian voice.

"Count off!" Coffin Ed yelled.

Both of them drew their pistols at the same time and put

a fusillade into the ceiling, which was already filled with holes they'd shot into it before.

The sudden shooting in the jammed room scared hell out of prisoners and cops alike. Everybody froze.

"As you were!" Grave Digger shouted.

He and Coffin Ed pushed their prisoners through the silent pack toward the desk.

The Harlem hoodlums under arrest looked at them from the corners of their eyes.

"Don't make graves," Grave Digger cautioned.

The lieutenant in charge glanced out briefly from the precinct captain's office behind the desk, but everything was quiet.

Goldy slipped unobtrusively into the room and stood just inside the doorway, stopping all the bail bondsmen who passed him with a jangle of his collection box.

"Give to the Lawd, gentlemen. Give to the poor."

If there was anything strange about a black Sister of Mercy soliciting in a Harlem precinct police station at one o'clock in the morning, no one remarked it.

Coffin Ed and Grave Digger got their prisoners booked immediately and handed them over to the jailor. The captain wanted to keep them in the street, not tied up all night in the station.

When they left, Goldy climbed into the back of their small black sedan and left with them. They parked the car in the dark on 127the Street and Grave Digger turned around.

"All right, what's the tip about the frogs?"

" 'Blessed is he that watcheth—' " Goldy began quoting.

Grave Digger cut him off. "Can that Bible-quoting crap. We let you operate because you're a stooly, and that's all. And don't you forget, we know you, Bud."

"Know everything there is to know about you," Coffin Ed added. "And I hate a goddam female inpersonator worse than God hates sin. So just give, Bud, give."

Goldy dropped his pose and talked straight.

"There's three con men operating here that's wanted in Mississippi on a murder rap."

"We know that much already," Grave Digger said. "Just

give us the monickers they're using and tell us where they're holed up."

"Two of them go as Morgan and Walker. I don't know the slim stud's handle. And I don't know where they're holed up. They're working the lost-gold-mine pitch and they're using a shill named Gus Parsons to bring in the suckers blindfolded."

"Where did you make them?"

"At Big Kathy's. Morgan and Walker were there tonight."

"Fill it in, fill it in," Grave Digger said harshly.

"I got a brother named Jackson, works for Exodus Clay. They took him for fifteen C's on The Blow. His old lady, Imabelle, tricked him into it, then she ran away with the slim stud."

"She's up with the gold-mine pitch?"

"Must be."

"What are they using for gold ore?"

"They got a few phony rocks."

Grave Digger turned to Coffin Ed. "We can take them at Big Kathy's."

"I got a better plan," Goldy said. "I'm goin' to load Jackson with a phony roll and let Gus Parsons contact him. Gus'll take him in to their headquarters and you-all can follow them."

Grave Digger shook his head. "You just said they took Jackson on The Blow."

"But Gus wasn't with them. Gus don't know Jackson. By the time Gus finds out his mistake you'll have the collar on them all."

Grave Digger and Coffin Ed exchanged looks. Coffin Ed nodded.

"Okay, Bud, we'll take them tomorrow night," Grave Digger said, then added grimly, "I suppose you're your brother's beneficiary."

"I'm just tryin' to help him, that's all," Goldy protested. "He wants his woman back."

"I'll bet," Coffin Ed said.

They let Goldy out of the car and drove off.

"Isn't there a warrant out for Jackson?" Coffin Ed remarked.

"Yeah, stole five hundred dollars from his boss."

"We'll take him too."

"We'll take them all."

The next afternoon when Jackson had finished eating, Goldy gave him a fill-in on the gang's setup and told him his plan to trap them.

"And here's the bait."

He made a huge roll out of stage money, encircled it with two bona fide ten-dollar bills, and bound it with an elastic band. That was the way jokers in Harlem carried their money when they wanted to big-time. He tossed it onto the table.

"Put that in your pocket, Bruzz, and you're goin' to be one big fat black piece of cheese. You're goin' to look like the biggest piece of cheese them rats ever seen."

Jackson looked at the phony roll without touching it.

He didn't like any part of Goldy's plan. Anything could go wrong. If there was a rumpus the detectives might grab him and let the real criminals go, like that phony marshal had done. Of course, these were real detectives. But they were colored detectives just the same. And from what he'd heard about them, they believed in shooting first and questioning the bodies afterward.

"Course if you don't want your gal back—" Goldy prodded.

Jackson picked up the phony roll and slipped it into his side pants-pocket. Then he crossed himself and knelt beside the table on the floor. Devoutly bowing his head, he whispered a prayer.

"Dear Lord in heaven, if You can't see fit to help this poor sinner in his hour of need, please don't help those dirty murderers either."

"What are you prayin' for, man?" Goldy said. "Ain't nothin' can happen to you. You goin' to be covered."

"That's what I'm worrying about," Jackson said. "I don't want to get covered too deep. . . ."

CHAPTER 10

THE BRADDOCK BAR was on the corner of 126th Street and Eighth Avenue, next door to a Negro-owned loan and insurance company and the Harlem weekly newspaper.

It had an expensive-looking front, small English-type windows with diamond-shaped leaded panes. Once it had claimed respectability, had been patronized by the white and colored businessmen in the neighborhood and their respectable employees. But when the whorehouses, gambling clubs, dope dens had taken over 126th Street to prey on the people from 125th Street, it had gone into bad repute.

"This bar has gone from sugar to shit," Jackson muttered to himself when he arrived there at seven o'clock.

The cold snowy February night was already getting liquored up.

Jackson squeezed into a place before the long bar, ordered a shot of rye, and looked at his neighbors nervously.

The bar was jammed with the lowest Harlem types, pinched-faced petty hustlers, sneak thieves, pickpockets, muggers, dope pushers, big rough workingmen in overalls and leather jackets. Everyone looked mean or dangerous.

Three hefty bartenders patrolled the sloppy floor behind, silently filling shot glasses and collecting coins.

A jukebox at the front was blaring, a whiskey-voice was shouting, *"Rock me, daddy, eight to the beat. Rock me, daddy, from my head to my feet."*

Goldy had instructed Jackson to flash his roll as soon as he'd ordered his first drink, but Jackson didn't have the nerve. He felt that everyone was watching him. He ordered a second drink. Then he noticed that everyone was watching everyone else, as though each one regarded his neighbor as either a potential victim or a stool pigeon for the police.

"Everybody in here lookin' for something, ain't they?" the man next to him said.

Jackson gave a start. "Looking for something?"

"See them whores, they're looking for a trick. See them muggers ganged around the door, they looking for a drunk to roll. These jokers in here are just waiting for a man to flash his money."

"Seems like I've seen you before," Jackson said. "Your name ain't Gus Parsons, is it?"

The man looked at Jackson suspiciously and began moving away. "What you want to know my name for?"

"I just thought I knew you," Jackson said, fingering the roll in his pocket, trying to get up enough courage to flash it.

He was saved for the moment by a fight.

Two rough-looking men jumped about the floor, knocking over chairs and tables, cutting at one another with switchblade knives. The customers at the bar screwed their heads about to watch, but held on to their places and kept their hands on their drinks. The whores rolled their eyes and looked bored.

One joker slashed the other's arm. A big-lipped wound opened in the tight leather jacket, but nothing came out but old clothes—two sweaters, three shirts, a pair of winter underwear. The second joker slashed back, opened a wound in the front of his foe's canvas jacket. But all that came out of the wound was dried printer's ink from the layers of old newspapers the joker had wrapped about him to keep warm. They kept slashing away at one another like two rag dolls battling in buck-dancing fury, spilling old clothes and last week's newsprint instead of blood.

The customers laughed.

"How them studs goin' to get cut?" someone remarked. "Might as well be fightin' old ragman's bag."

65

"They ain't doin' nothin' but cheatin' the Salvation Army."

"They ain't tryin' to cut each other, man. Them studs know each other. They just tryin' to freeze each other to death."

One of the bartenders went out with a sawed-off baseball bat and knocked one of the fighters on the head. When that one fell the other one leaned down to cut him again and the bartender knocked him on the head also.

Two white cops strolled in lazily, as though they had smelled the fight, and took the battlers away.

Jackson thought it might be safe then to flash his roll. He took out the phony bills, carefully peeled off a ten, threw it onto the bar.

"Take out for two rye whiskeys," he said.

A dead silence fell. Every eye in the joint looked at the roll in his hand, then looked at him, then at the bartender.

The bartender held the bill up to the light, peered through it, turned it over and snapped it between his hands, then he rang it up in the register and slammed the change onto the bar.

"What you want to do, get your throat cut?" he said angrily.

"What you want me to do, walk off without paying?" Jackson argued.

"I just don't want no trouble in here," the bartender said, but it was too late for that.

Underworld characters closed in on Jackson from all sides. But the whores got there first, pressing their wares so hard against Jackson he couldn't tell whether they were soliciting or trying to dispose of surplus merchandise. The pickpockets were trying to break through. The muggers waited at the door. Everyone else watched him, curious and attentive.

"That's my money," a big whiskey-headed ex-pug shouted, pushing through the crowd toward Jackson. "That mother— has done picked my pocket."

Someone laughed.

66

"Don't let that joker scare you, honey," one of the whores encouraged.

Another one said, "That raggedy stud ain't had two white quarters since Jesus was a child."

"I don't want no trouble in here," the bartender warned, reaching for his sawed-off bat.

"I know my money," the ex-pug shouted. "Can't nobody tell me I don't know my own money."

"What's the difference between your money and anybody else's money?" the bartender said.

A medium-sized, brown-skinned man, dressed in a camel's-hair coat, brown beaver hat, hard-finished brown-and-white striped suit, brown suede shoes, brown silk tie decorated with hand-painted yellow horses, wearing a diamond ring on his left ring-finger and a gold signet-ring on his right hand, carrying gloves in his left hand, swinging his right hand free, pushed open the street door and came into the bar fast. He stopped short on seeing the ex-pug grab Jackson by the shoulder. He heard the ex-pug say in a threatening voice, "Leave me see that mother-rapin' roll." He noticed the two bartenders close in for action. He saw the whores backing away. He cased the situation instantly. Pushing his way through the jam, he walked up behind the ex-pug, took hold of his arm, spun him about and kicked him solidly in the groin.

The big ex-pug doubled forward, blowing spit in a loud grunt. The man stepped back and kicked him in the solar plexus. The ex-pug's face ballooned as he gasped for breath, folding head-downward toward the floor. The man stepped back another pace and kicked him in the face with the curve of his instep, hard enough to close one eye without breaking any bones, and timed so that the ex-pug fell on his chest instead of his face. Then the man daintily inserted the tip of his brown suede shoe underneath the ex-pug's shoulder and flipped him over onto his back. Slowly he stuck his right hand into the side pocket of his overcoat and pulled out a short-barreled .38 police special revolver.

The customers scattered, getting out of range.

"You're the son of a bitch who robbed me last night," the man said to the half-conscious ex-pug on the floor. "I've got a good notion to blow out your guts."

He had a good voice and spoke in a soft, slow manner that made him sound like an educated man, to the customers in that joint.

"Don't shoot him in here, Mister," one of the bartenders said.

At sight of the gun the ex-pug's eyeballs rolled back in his head so that only the whites showed. He kept swallowing his tongue as he tried to talk.

"Twarn't me, Boss," he finally managed to blubber. "I swear 'fore the cross it warn't me. I ain't never tried to rob you, Boss."

"The hell it wasn't you. I'd know you anywhere. You jumped me on 129th Street right after midnight last night."

"I swear it warn't me, Boss. I been right here in this bar all last night. Joe the bartender'll tell you. I been right here all last night. Didn't leave no time."

"That's right," the bartender said. "He was here all last night. I seen him."

The ex-pug wallowed about the floor, feeling his eye and groaning as though half dead, trying to win sympathy.

The man put away his gun and said evenly, "Well, you son of a bitch, I might be mistaken this time. But you've sure as hell robbed somebody in your lifetime, so you just got what was due you."

The ex-pug got to his feet and backed away a distance.

"I wouldn't rob you, Boss, no suh, not with what you got."

No one thought it was funny but they all laughed.

"Not you, Boss, not a man of your position," the ex-pug kept clowning for laughs. "Anybody here will tell you I ain't had no real money in my pockets for weeks." Suddenly he recalled that he'd just accused Jackson of picking his pocket, and added, "Maybe it was that man at the bar what robbed you, boss. He's sportin' a big roll he got from somewheres."

The man looked at Jackson for the first time.

"Listen, don't get me into that," Jackson said. "I hit the numbers for my money. I can prove it."

The man went over and stood beside Jackson at the bar and ordered a drink.

"Don't worry, friend, I know it wasn't you," he said in a friendly voice. "It was some big ragged mugger like that bastard there. But I'll find him."

"How much did you lose?"

"Seven hundred dollars," the man said, turning the shot glass between his fingers. "If that had happened to me a week ago, I'd have tracked the bastard to hell. But now it don't make too much difference. I've lucked up on a good thing since then, something that's solid gold. Eight or nine months from now I'll be able to give a bastard that much money just to keep from having to kill him."

At the word *gold*, Jackson looked up quickly at the reflection of the man in the mirror behind the bar. He ordered another drink, pulled out his roll and peeled off a bill to pay for it.

The man eyed Jackson's roll.

"Friend, if I was you I wouldn't flash my money in this joint. That's just asking for trouble."

"I don't usually come in here," Jackson said. "But my woman's not at home right now."

The man gave Jackson a poker-faced look. He'd gotten a tip from one of the cheap hustlers he employed as lookouts that a square loaded with a big roll was in the joint. But Jackson looked too much like a square to be a real square. The man wondered if Jackson was trying to rook him with a confidence game of his own. He decided to go slow.

"I figured that," he said noncommittally.

The whores began closing in on Jackson again and the man beckoned to the bartender.

"Give these whores what they're drinking and get them off my back."

The bartender took a bottle of gin and a tray of shot

glasses to one of the booths. The whores melted away from the bar, looking hostile but as though they couldn't be so much bothered as to be offended.

"You shouldn't talk that way to women," Jackson protested.

The man looked at Jackson queerly. "What can you call a two-bit whore but a whore, friend?"

"They were good enough for Jesus to save," Jackson said.

The man grinned with relief. Jackson was his boy.

"You're right, friend. I'm upset a little, don't usually talk like that. My name's Gus Parsons." He stuck out his hand. "I'm in the real-estate business."

Jackson shook hands, also relieved.

"Glad to meet you, Gus. They call me Jackson."

"What business are you in, Jackson?"

"I'm in the undertaking business."

Gus laughed. "Business must be good, considering that roll you're carrying around. How much are you carrying there, anyway?"

"It didn't come from my business. I just work for an undertaker. I hit the numbers."

"That's right. You did say you'd had a hit."

"Had twenty dollars on four eleven. I drew down ten thousand dollars."

Gus whistled softly and looked suddenly serious.

"You take my advice, Jackson, keep that roll in your pocket and go straight home. The streets of Harlem are not safe for a man with that kind of money. You'd better let me go along with you until you see a policeman."

He turned and called to the bartender. "How much do I owe?"

"Let me buy you a drink before we leave," Jackson said.

"You can buy me a drink somewhere else if you want, Jackson," Gus said, paying for his drink and the bottle of gin. "Some place that's clean and where a man can feel safe. Let's get away from these hoodlums and thieves. I tell you, let's walk down to the Palm Café."

"That's fine," Jackson said.

70

CHAPTER 11

THEY TURNED on 125th Street and walked toward Seventh Avenue. Neon lights from the bars and stores threw multicolored rays on the multicolored people trudging down the sloppy walk, turning their complexions into strange metallic shades. Colored men passed, bundled against the cold, some in new checked overcoats, others in GI rubber slickers, gabardines, coats that looked as though they'd been made from blankets. Colored women switched by, sporting coats of such unlikely fur as horse, bear, buffalo, cow, dog, cat, and even bat. Other colored people were dressed in cashmere, melton, mink and muskrat. They drove past in big new cars, looking prosperous.

A Sister of Mercy emerged from the shadows.

"Give to the Lawd. Give to the poor."

Jackson reached for his roll, but Gus stopped him.

"Keep you money hidden, Jackson. I have some change."

He dropped a half-dollar into the box.

" 'Ye have found the Spirit,' " the Sister of Mercy misquoted. " 'He that hath an ear, let him hear what the Spirit sayeth.' "

"Amen," Jackson said.

Near the intersection of Seventh Avenue they turned into the Palm Café. The bartenders wore starched white jackets, and the high-yellow waitresses plying between the tables and booths were dressed in green-and-yellow uniforms. A three-piece combo beat out hot rhythms on the raised bandstand.

The customers were the hepped-cats who lived by their

wits—smooth Harlem hustlers with shiny straightened hair, dressed in lurid elegance, along with their tightly draped queens, chorus girls and models—which meant anything—sparkling with iridescent glass jewelry, rolling dark mascaraed eyes, flashing crimson fingernails, smiling with pearl-white teeth encircled by purple-red lips, exhibiting the hot excitement that money could buy.

Gus pushed to the bar and drew Jackson in beside him.

"This is the kind of place I like," he said. "I like culture. Good food. Fine wine. Prosperous men. Beautiful women. Cosmopolitan atmosphere. Only trouble is, it takes money, Jackson, money."

"Well, I got the money," Jackson said, beckoning to the bartender. "What are you drinking?"

Both ordered Scotch.

Then Gus said, "Not your kind of money, Jackson. You haven't got enough money to keep up this kind of life. I mean real money. You take your little money. If you're not careful it'll be gone inside of six months. What I mean is money that don't have any end."

"I know what you mean," Jackson said. "As soon as my woman buys herself a fur coat and I get myself some new clothes and we get ourselves a car, a Buick or something like that, we'll be stone broke. But where's a man going to get money that don't have any end?"

"Jackson, you impress me as being an honest man."

"I try to be, but honesty don't always pay."

"Yes it does, Jackson. You've just got to know how to make it pay."

"I sure wish I knew."

"Jackson, I've a good mind to let you in on something good. A deal that will make you some real money. The kind of money I'm talking about. The only thing is, I've got to be sure I can trust you to keep quiet about it."

"Oh, I can keep quiet. If there's any way I can make some real money I can keep so quiet they'll call me oyster-mouth."

"Come on, Jackson, let's go back here where we can talk privately," Gus said suddenly, taking Jackson by the arm and steering him to a table in the rear. "I'm going to buy you a dinner and as soon as this girl takes our order I'm going to show you something."

The waitress came over and stood beside their table, looking off in another direction.

"Are you waiting on us or just waiting on us to get up and leave?" Gus asked.

She gave him a scornful look. "Just state your order and we'll fill it."

Gus looked her over, beginning at her feet. "Bring us some steaks, girlie, and be sure they're not as tough as you are, and take the lip away."

"Two steak dinners," she said angrily, switching away.

"Lean this way," Gus said to Jackson, and drew a sheaf of stock certificates decorated with gold seals and Latin script from his inside coat pocket. He spread them out beneath the edge of the table for Jackson to get a better view.

"You see these, Jackson? They're shares in a Mexican gold mine. They're going to make me rich."

Jackson stretched his eyes as wide as possible. "A gold mine, you say?"

"A real eighteen-carat gold mine, Jackson. And the richest mine in this half of the world. A colored man discovered it, and a colored man has formed a corporation to operate it, and they're selling stock just to us colored people like you and me. It's a closed corporation. You can't beat that."

The waitress brought the steak dinners, but Jackson couldn't eat very much. He had eaten not long before, but Gus thought it was due to excitement.

"Don't get so excited you can't eat, Jackson. You can't enjoy your money if you're dead."

"I know that's true, but I was just thinking. I sure would like to invest my money in some of those shares, Mr. Parsons."

"Just call me Gus, Jackson," Gus said. "You don't have to shine up to me. I can't sell you any shares. You have to see Mr. Morgan, the financier who's organizing the corporation. He's the man who sells the stock. All I can do is recommend you. If they don't think you're worthy to own stock in the corporation, he won't sell you any. You can bet on that. He only wants respectable people to own shares in his corporation."

"Will you recommend me, Gus? If you have any doubts about me, I can get a letter from my minister."

"That won't be necessary, Jackson. I can tell that you are an honest, upright citizen. I pride myself on being a good judge of character. A man in my business—the real-estate business—has got to be a good judge of character or he won't be in business long. How much do you want to invest, Jackson?"

"All of it," Jackson said. "The whole ten thousand."

"In that case I'll take you to see Mr. Morgan right now. They'll be working all night tonight, clearing up business here so tomorrow they can go on to Philadelphia and let a few good citizens there buy shares too. They want to give worthy colored people from all over the country a chance to share in the profits that will come from this mine."

"I can understand that," Jackson said.

When they left the Palm Café the same Sister of Mercy who had accosted them before was shuffling past, and turned to give them a saintly smile.

"Give to the Lawd. Give to the poor. Pave your way to heaven with charitable coins. Think of the unfortunate."

Gus fished out another half-dollar. "I got it, Jackson."

"Sister Gabriel blesses you, brother. 'And the Lord of the spirits of the prophets sent his angel to show unto his servants the things which must shortly come to pass. And behold, we come quickly. Blessed is he that keepeth the word of the prophecy.' "

Gus turned away impatiently.

Goldy winked at Jackson and formed words with his lips. "You dig me, Bruzz?"

"Amen," Jackson said.

"I'm suspicious about those nuns," Gus said as he led Jackson toward his car. "Has it ever occurred to you that they might be working a racket?"

"How can you think that about Sisters of Mercy?" Jackson protested quickly. He didn't want Gus to start suspecting Goldy before the trap was sprung. "They're the most holy people in Harlem."

Gus laughed apologetically. "In my business—the real-estate business—so many people try crooked dealings a man gets to be suspicious. Then I'm naturally a skeptic to begin with. I don't believe in anything until I know it's for sure. That's the way I felt about this gold mine. I had to be sure about it before I invested my money. But I can see that you're a church man, Jackson."

"Member of the First Baptist Church," Jackson said.

"You don't have to tell me, Jackson, I could see right from the start that you were a church member. That's how I knew you were an honest man."

He stopped beside a lavender-colored Cadillac. "Here's my car."

"The real-estate business must be good," Jackson said, climbing into the front seat beside Gus.

"You can't always tell by a Cadillac, Jackson," Gus said as he pushed the starter button and shifted the hydromatic clutch. "All you need these days to buy a Cadillac is a jalopy to turn in for a down payment, and then dodge the installment collector."

Jackson laughed and glanced into the rear-view mirror. He noticed a small black sedan turn the corner and fall in behind them. Then after a moment a taxi drew suddenly to the curb where they had left Goldy.

"When I get the first payment from my mine shares I'm going to buy me one of these."

"Don't count your chickens before they hatch, Jackson. Mr. Morgan hasn't sold you any shares yet."

Suddenly, when they had rounded the corner at St. Nicholas Avenue, heading north, Gus drew to the curb and stopped. Jackson noticed the black sedan turn the corner, slow down, then drive on. It was followed at a short distance by a taxi. Gus didn't notice. He had taken a black hood from the glove compartment.

"Sorry, Jackson, but I've got to blindfold you," he said.

"You just slip this over your head. You understand, Mr. Morgan and the prospector have got a hundred thousand dollars' worth of gold ore in their office and they can't take any chances of being robbed."

Jackson hesitated. "It's not that, Mr. Parsons. It's just that, well, you see, I got all this money on me—"

Gus laughed. "Call me Gus, Jackson. And don't hesitate to say what you mean."

"It's not that I don't trust you, Gus, but—"

"I understand, Jackson. You just met me and you don't know me from the man in the moon. Here, take my gun if it makes you feel any safer."

"Well, it's not that I don't feel safe with you, Gus—" Jackson said, taking the gun and slipping it into his right-hand overcoat pocket. "It's just that—"

"Say no more about it, Jackson," Gus said as he pulled the hood down over Jackson's head. "I know just how an honest man like you feels in this situation. But it can't be helped."

With the hood over his head, Jackson was suddenly scared. He put his hand on the gun for reassurance and silently prayed that Goldy knew what he was doing.

He heard the motor purr and the car move. It turned corner after corner. He tried to estimate their direction, but they turned so many corners he became confused.

Half an hour later the car slowed down and stopped. Jackson had no idea where he was.

"Well, here we are, Jackson, safe and sound," Gus said. "Nothing has happened to you. You just keep your mask on a little while longer and we'll be inside of the office, face to face with Mr. Morgan. You just give me my pistol now; you won't need it any more."

Jackson felt the sweat break out on his head and face beneath the mask. The street was silent. There were no sounds of approaching cars. If Gus had lost the detectives and Goldy, who were supposed to be following, then he was in trouble.

He reached for the pistol with his right hand and with his left hand jerked off the mask. All he had time to see was the quick movement of Gus's hand that had been resting on the steering wheel, before Gus's fist exploded on his nose, filling his vision with dripping wet stars. He put his head down and rammed toward Gus like a fat bull, trying to pin Gus down with his bulk and draw the pistol at the same time. But Gus jabbed him in the windpipe with the point of his right elbow and clutched his wrist in a steel grip before he could get the pistol from his pocket. The dripping wet stars in Jackson's vision turned into blood-red balloons the size of watermelons.

CHAPTER 12

THE BLACK SEDAN came up so fast it skidded to a stop slantwise, and the two big loose-jointed colored detectives wearing shabby gray overcoats and misshapen snap-brim hats hit the pavement on each side in a flatfooted lope.

At the same moment Goldy's taxi pulled to the curb and parked a block down the street, but Goldy didn't get out.

When the two detectives converged on the flashy Cadillac they had their long-barreled nickel-plated pistols in their hands. Coffin Ed opened the door and Grave Digger hauled Gus to the pavement.

"Get your God-damned hands off me," Gus snarled, throwing a looping right-hand punch at Grave Digger's face.

Grave Digger pulled back from the punch and said, "Just slap him, Ed."

Coffin Ed slapped Gus on the cheek with his open palm. Gus's tight-fitting hat sailed off and he spun toward Grave Digger, who slapped him on the other cheek and spun him back toward Coffin Ed. They slapped him fast, from one to another, like batting a Ping-pong ball. Gus's head began ringing. He lost his sense of balance and his legs began to buckle. They slapped him until he fell to his knees, deaf to the world.

Coffin Ed grabbed the collar of his overcoat to keep him from falling on his face. He knelt limply between them with his bare head lolling forward. Grave Digger lifted his chin with the barrel of his pistol. Coffin Ed looked at Grave Digger over Gus's head.

"Tender?"

"Any more tender and he'd be chopped meat," Grave Digger said.

"This boy wasn't educated right."

Jackson hadn't moved from his seat while the detectives were working on Gus, but suddenly he opened the far door and got out on the sidewalk, hoping he could get away unnoticed.

"Hold on, Bud, we're not finished with you yet," Grave Digger called.

"Yes, sir," Jackson said meekly. "I was just getting ready to see what you wanted me to do."

"We still have to get inside the joint."

"Yes, sir."

"Let's get this boy together, Ed."

Coffin Ed lifted Gus to his feet and put a pint bottle of bourbon into his hand. Gus took a drink and choked, but his ears popped and he could hear again. His legs were still wobbly, as though he were punch-drunk.

Coffin Ed took the bottle and slipped it back into his overcoat pocket. "Do you want to cooperate now?" he asked Gus.

"I ain't got no choice," Gus said.

"That's not the right attitude."

"Easy, Ed," Grave Digger cautioned. "We're not through with this boy yet. He's got to get us inside."

"That's what I mean," Coffin Ed said, looking about at his surroundings. "It's a hell of a place to make a pitch on a con game."

"They picked it for the getaway. They figure it's hard to get them cornered here."

"We'll see."

Overhead was the 155th Street Bridge, crossing the Harlem River from Coogan's Bluff on Manhattan Island to that flat section of the Bronx where the Yankee Stadium is located. The Polo Grounds loomed in the dark on a flat strip between the sheer bluff and the Harlem River. The iron stanchions beneath the bridge were like ghostly sentinels in the impenetrable gloom. A spur of the Bronx elevated line crossed the river in the distance connecting with the station near the Stadium gates.

It was a dark, deserted, dismal section of Manhattan, eerie, shunned and unpatrolled at night, where a man could get his throat cut in perfect isolation with no one to hear his cries and no one brave enough to answer them if he did.

Gus's Cadillac was parked directly in front of a huge warehouse that had been converted into a Peace Heaven by Father Divine. The word PEACE appeared in huge white letters on each side of the gabled roof, and could be seen only by looking down from the bridge. It had later been abandoned and was now sealed in darkness.

"I'd sure hate to be here alone," Jackson said.

"Don't worry, son, we got you covered," Grave Digger reassured him. He locked Gus's Cadillac and put the key into his pocket.

"Okay, Bud, get your hat and let's get going," Coffin Ed said to Gus.

Gus picked up his hat, straightened it out and put it on. His face had already swollen so much that his eyes were almost closed.

"Just act as if nothing happened," Grave Digger ordered.

"That ain't going to be easy to do," Gus complained.

"Bud, you'd better make it good, easy or not."

"Well, coppers, here we go," Gus said.

He led them down a narrow dark alleyway beside the abandoned Heaven to a small wooden shack on the bank of the river. It was painted a dark, dull green but looked black at night. There were two shuttered windows on the side visible from the walk, and a heavy wooden door at the front. No light showed from within; no sound was heard but the distant chug-chug of tug boats towing garbage scows down the river and out to the sea.

Coffin Ed motioned to Gus with his pistol.

Gus rapped a signal on the door. He rapped at such length that Coffin Ed tensed. The slight click of his pistol being cocked shattered the silence like a giant firecracker exploding, causing Jackson to jump halfway out of his skin.

Suddenly a Judas window opened in the black door. Jackson's heart tried to fly out of his mouth. Then he found himself looking directly into an eye staring from the Judas window. He couldn't see the eye well enough to recognize it, but it seemed to speak to him.

There was a turning of locks and a drawing of bolts, and the door opened outward.

Now Jackson could see the eye and its mate plainly. A high-yellow sensual face was framed in the light of the door. It was Imabelle's face. She was looking steadily into Jackson's eyes. Her lips formed the words, "Come on in and kill him, Daddy. I'm all yours." Then she stepped back, making space for him to enter.

Her words shocked Jackson. He crossed himself involuntarily. He wanted to speak to her but he couldn't get the handle to his voice. He looked at her pleadingly, tried to swallow and couldn't make it, then stepped into the room.

It was a single room, about the size of a two-car garage. There were two shuttered windows on each side and another door at the rear, which was locked and bolted. It might have been a foreman's office or a timekeeper's bureau for some firm operating on the river.

To one side of the rear door were a large flat-topped desk and a swivel chair. Two cheap overstuffed chairs, three straight-backed wooden chairs, ashstands, a glass-topped cocktail table, a tin filing-cabinet, and a phony cardboard safe covered with black canvas so that only the bottom half of the dial could be distinguished in the dim light in the corner, had obviously been added as props by the confidence gang. This was to create an atmosphere of luxuriousness and comfort to impress the suckers while they were being trimmed. Light came from a floor lamp between the armchairs, a ceiling lamp in a glass globe, and a green-shaded desk-lamp.

Looking past Imabelle, Jackson saw Hank sitting behind the desk, his yellow face looking corpse-like in the green upper glow from the desk-lamp.

Jodie sat on a campstool beside the back door, dressed in high laced boots and dungarees. His straightened hair was gray with dust. All he needed was a scabby burro to give the illusion of coming down a mountain trail loaded with gold nuggets.

Slim sat in a straight-backed chair against the wall beside the desk, wearing over his suit a long khaki duster like those worn by mad scientists in low-budget horror motion pictures. The legend *U. S. Assayer* was embroidered on the chest.

At sight of Jackson all three sat bolt upright and stared.

Before anyone could move, Grave Digger put his foot against Gus's back and shoved him into the room with such force that he catapulted across the floor and rammed headfirst into Jackson's back. Jackson was knocked forward into Jodie just as Jodie was rising from his campstool. Jodie was pinned against the wall.

Following close behind, Grave Digger shouted, "Straighten up!"

Coffin Ed sealed up the open doorway with his cocked .38 and echoed, "Count off!"

Slim jumped to his feet with his hands elevated. Hank sat frozen with his hands on the desk top. Momentarily shielded from the detectives' guns by Jackson's body, Jodie punched Jackson twice, hard, in the belly.

Jackson grunted and grabbed Jodie by the throat. Jodie kneed Jackson in the groin. Jackson backed painfully into Gus. Gus grabbed Jackson by the shoulder to keep from falling, but Jackson thought Gus was trying to hold him and twisted violently from his grip.

In a blind rage, Jodie whipped out his switchblade knife and slashed open the sleeve of Jackson's overcoat.

"Drop it!" Grave Digger shouted.

Red-eyed with pain and fury, Jackson kicked Jodie on the shin as Jodie drew back the knife to stab at him again.

Imabelle saw the poised knife and screamed, "Look out, Daddy!"

Her scream was so piercing that everyone except that two detectives ducked involuntarily. It even scratched the case-hardened nerves of Grave Digger. His finger tightened spasmodically on the hair trigger of his pistol and the explosion of the shot in the small room deafened everyone.

Gus had ducked into the line of fire and the .38 bullet penetrated his skull back of the left ear and came out over the right eye. As he fell dying, Gus made one more grab at Jackson, but Jackson leaped aside like a shying horse, and Jodie grappled with him.

Jackson clutched Jodie's wrist and tried to swing him about into Grave Digger's reach, but Jodie outpowered him and backed Jackson toward Grave Digger instead.

Taking advantage of the commotion, Hank snatched up a glass of acid sitting on the desk. The acid had been used to demonstrate the purity of the gold ore, and Hank saw his chance to throw it into Coffin Ed's eyes.

Imabelle saw him and screamed again, "Look out!"

Everybody ducked again. Jackson and Jodie butted heads accidentally. By dodging, Slim came between Coffin Ed and Hank just as Hank threw the acid and Coffin Ed shot. Some of the acid splashed on Slim's ear and neck; the rest splashed into Coffin Ed's face. Coffin Ed's shot went wild and shattered the desk-lamp.

Slim jumped backward so violently he slammed against the wall.

Hank dropped behind the desk a fraction of a second before Coffin Ed, blinded with the burning acid and a white-hot rage, emptied his pistol, spraying the top of the desk and the wall behind it with .38 slugs.

One of the bullets hit a hidden light-switch and plunged the room into darkness.

"Easy does it," Grave Digger shouted in warning, and backed toward the door to cut off escape.

Coffin Ed didn't know the lights were out. He was a tough man. He had to be a tough man to be a colored detective in Harlem. He closed his eyes against the burning pain, but he was so consumed with rage that he began clubbing right and left in the dark with the butt of his pistol.

83

He didn't know it was Grave Digger who backed into him. He just felt somebody within reach and he clubbed Grave Digger over the head with such savage fury that he knocked him unconscious. Grave Digger crumpled to the floor at the same instant that Coffin Ed was asking in the dark, "Where are you, Digger? Where are you, man?"

For a moment the speechless dark was filled with violent commotion. Bodies collided in a desperate race for the door. There was the sound of crashing objects and shattering glass as the floor lamp and cocktail table were overturned and trampled.

Then Imabelle screamed again, "Don't you cut me!"

A rage-thickened voice spluttered, "I'll kill you, you double-crossing bitch."

Jackson lunged toward the sound of Imabelle's voice to protect her.

"Where are you, Digger? Speak up, man," Coffin Ed yelled, groping in the dark. Despite the unendurable pain, his first duty was to his partner.

"Let her alone, she ain't done it," another voice said.

A furious struggle broke out between Jodie and Slim. Jackson realized that one of them thought Imabelle had ratted to the cops and was trying to kill her. The other one objected. He couldn't tell which was which.

He plunged toward the sound of the scuffling, prepared to fight both. Instead he landed in the arms of Coffin Ed. The next moment he was knocked unconscious by a pistol butt laid against his skull.

"Are you hurt, Digger?" Coffin Ed asked anxiously, stumbling over Grave Digger's unconscious body in the dark. "Are you hurt, man?"

"Come on, let's go!" Hank yelled and made a running leap through the doorway.

Imabelle ran out behind him.

Suddenly, by unspoken accord, Slim and Jodie stopped fighting to chase Imabelle. But outside, where they could see better, they squared off again. Both had open knives and began slashing furiously at each other, but cutting only the cold night air.

84

Behind the house, an outboard motor coughed and coughed again. The third time it coughed the motor caught. Jodie broke away from Slim and ran around the side of the shack. A moment later a boat with an outboard motor roared out into the Harlem River.

Slim clutched Imabelle by the arm.

"Come on, let's scram, they done left us," he said, pulling her up the alley toward the street.

Suddenly the night was filled with the screaming of sirens as four patrol cars began converging on the spot. A motorist passing over the 155th Street Bridge had reported hearing shooting on the Harlem River and the cops were coming on like General Sherman tanks.

Coffin Ed heard them like an answer to a prayer. The furiously burning pain had become almost more than he could bear. He hadn't reloaded his gun for fear of blowing out his brains. Now he began blowing on his police whistle as though he had gone mad. He blew it so long and loud it brought Jackson back to consciousness.

Grave Digger was still out.

Coffin Ed heard Jackson clambering to his feet and quickly reloaded his pistol. Jackson heard bullets clicking into the cylinder slots and felt his flesh crawl.

"Who's there?" Coffin Ed challenged.

His voice sounded so loud and harsh Jackson gave a start and lost his voice.

"Speak up, God damn it, or I'll blow you in two," Coffin Ed threatened.

"It's just me, Jackson, Mr. Johnson," Jackson managed to say.

"Jackson! Where the hell is everybody, Jackson?"

"They all done got away 'cept me."

"Where's my buddy? Where's Digger Jones?"

"I don't know, sir. I ain't seen him."

"Maybe he's gone after them. But you stay right where you are, Jackson. Don't you move a goddam step."

"No, sir. Is there any kind of way I can help you, sir?"

"No, God damn it, just don't move. You're under arrest."

"Yes, sir."

I might have known it, Jackson was thinking. The real criminals had gotten away again and he was the only one caught.

He began inching silently toward the doorway.

"Is that you I hear moving, Jackson?"

"No sir. It ain't me." Jackson moved a little closer. "I swear 'fore God." He inched a little closer. "Must be rats underneath the floor."

"Rats, all right, God damn it," Coffin Ed grated. "And they're going to be underneath the God damn ground before it's done with."

Through the open doorway Jackson could see alongside the abandoned Heaven of Father Divine the lights of the patrol cars moving back and forth, searching the street. He listened to the motors whining, the sirens screaming. He felt the presence of Coffin Ed behind him waving the cocked .38 in the pitch darkness of his blind eyes. The shrill, insistent blast of Coffin Ed's police whistle scraped layer after layer from Jackson's nerves. It sounded as if all hell had broken loose everywhere, top and bottom, on this side and that, and he was standing there between the devil and the deep blue sea.

Better to get shot running than standing, he decided. He crouched.

Coffin Ed sensed his movement.

"Are you still there, Jackson?" he barked.

Jackson sprang through the open doorway, landed on his hands and knees, and came up running.

"Jackson, you bastard!" he heard Coffin Ed screaming. "Holy jumping Moses, I can't take this much longer. Can't the sons of bitches hear? Jackson!" he yelled at the top of his voice.

Three shots blasted the night, the long red flame bursting the black darkness from the barrel of Coffin Ed's pistol. Jackson heard the bullets crashing through the wooden walls.

Jackson churned his knees in a froth of panic, trying to get greater speed from his short black legs. It pumped sweat from his pores, steam cooked him in his own juice, squandered his strength, upset his gait, but didn't increase his speed. In Harlem they say a lean man can't sit and a fat man can't run. He was trying to get to the other side of the old brick warehouse that had been converted into Heaven but it seemed as far off as the resurrection of the dead.

Behind him three more shots blasted the enclosing din, inspiring him like a burning rag on a dog's tail. He couldn't think of anything but an old folk song he'd learned in his youth:

> Run, nigger, run; de patter-roller catch you;
> Run, nigger, run; and try to get away . . .

His foot slipped on a muddy spot and he sailed head-on into the old wooden loading-dock at the back of the reconverted Heaven, invisible in the dark. His fat-cushioned mouth smacked into the edge of a heavy floorboard with the sound of meat slapping on a chopping block. Tears of pain flew from his eyes.

As he jumped back, licking his bruised lips, he heard the clatter of policemen's feet coming around the other side of the Heaven.

He crawled up over the edge of the dock like a clumsy crab escaping a snapping turtle. A ladder was within reach to his right, but he didn't see it.

Overhead the 155th Street Bridge hung across the dark night, strung with lighted cars slowing to a stop as passengers craned their necks to see the cause of the commotion.

A lone tugboat towing two empty garbage-scows chugged down the Harlem River to pick up garbage bound for the sea. Its green and red riding lights were reflected in shimmering doubletakes on the black river.

Jackson felt hemmed in on both sides; if the cops didn't get him the river would. He jumped to his feet and started to run again. His footsteps boomed like thunder in his ears on the rotten floorboards. A loose board gave beneath his foot and he plunged face forward on his belly.

A policeman rounding the other side of the Heaven,

coming in from the street, flashed his light in a wide searching arc. It passed over Jackson's prone figure, black against the black boards, and moved along the water's edge.

Jackson jumped up and began to run again. The old folk song kept beating in his head:

> Dis nigger run, he run his best,
> Stuck his head in a hornet's nest.

The tricky echo of the river and the buildings made his footsteps sound to the cops as coming from the opposite direction. Their lights flashed downriver as they converged in front of the wooden shack.

"God damn it, in here," Jackson heard Coffin Ed's roar.

"Coming," he heard the quick reply.

"Somebody's getting away," Jackson heard another voice shout. He put his feet down and picked them up as fast as he could, but it took him so long to get to the end of the dock he felt as if he'd turned stark white from old age and had withered half away.

From the corners of his white-walled eyes he saw the policemen's lights swinging back up the river, slowly closing in. And he didn't have anywhere to hide.

Suddenly he went off the edge of the dock without seeing it. He was running on wooden boards and the next thing he knew he was running on the cool night air. The next moment he was skidding into a puddle of muck. His feet went out from underneath him so fast he turned a complete somersault.

The lights passed along the platform overhead and swung back along the river's edge. He was shielded by the dock, safe for the moment in the shadows.

A passageway loomed to his left, a narrow opening between the brick walls of the Heaven and the corrugated zinc walls of an adjoining warehouse. Far down, another lifetime away, was a narrow rectangle of light where it came out into the street. He made for it, slipped in the muck, caught himself on his hands, and ran the first ten yards bear-fashion.

He straightened up when he felt the ground harden under his feet. He was in a narrow passageway; he had entered it so fast he was stuck before he knew it. He thrashed and wriggled in a blind panic, like a black Don Quixote fighting two big warehouses singlehanded; he got himself turned sideways, and ran crab-like toward the street.

The alley was clogged with tin cans, beer bottles, water-soaked cardboard cartons, pieces of wooden crates, and all other manner of trash. Jackson's shins took a beating; his overcoat was scraped by both walls as he propelled his fat body through the narrow opening, running in a strange sidewise motion, right foot leaping ahead, left foot dragging up behind.

He couldn't get that damn' song out of his mind. It was like a ghost haunting him:

> Dat nigger run, dat nigger flew
> Dat nigger tore his shirt in two.

CHAPTER 13

WHEN SLIM and Imabelle came out on the sidewalk, the first of the police cars was screaming up Eighth Avenue at ninety miles an hour, its red light blinking in the black night like a demon escaped from hell.

Slim's car was parked too far away to reach. He tried Gus's Cadillac and found it locked. Luckily there was a taxi parked at the curb, ahead of the Cadillac.

Slim looked at the Sister of Mercy sitting on the back seat and recognized her as the black nun who had been pointed out to him in front of Blumstein's Department Store as a stool pigeon. He jerked open the door, jumped inside first and pulled Imabelle in afterwards.

"This is an emergency," he shouted at the driver. "Knickerbocker Hospital, and goose it."

He turned to the nun and explained, "My wife drank some poison. Got to get her to the hospital."

The burns on Slim's cheek and neck were on the far side, but Goldy had already noticed the acid burns on the shoulder of his khaki duster and knew there had been acid throwing too. He had heard the shooting, and he figured with so much shooting by those crack shots Grave Digger and Coffin Ed, somebody had to be dead. He just hoped it wasn't Jackson, or he was going to have to figure out some way of getting the trunk by himself. And that was going to be tough, because Imabelle didn't know he was Jackson's brother.

The main thing at the moment was not to arouse their suspicions.

"Put your faith in the Lord," he whispered huskily, trying to give the impression of being simple-minded. "Let not your heart be troubled."

Slim shot him a suspicious look, and for an instant Goldy was afraid he'd overplayed it. But Slim only muttered, "Gonna be troubled if we don't get going."

Imabelle had run out without her coat and she shivered suddenly from cold.

Before the taxi had gotten into second gear, a patrol car cut in front of it. Slim cursed. Imabelle put her arm about Slim's shoulder and leaned her head against his cheek to hide the acid burns. Two cops leaped out, stalked back to the taxi and flashed their lights over the occupants. On seeing the Sister of Mercy, they saluted respectfully.

"Did you see anyone run past here, Sister?" one of them asked.

"No one has run past us," Goldy replied truthfully, and turned to his companions. "Did you see anybody pass us?"

"I ain't seen nobody," Slim corroborated quickly, shooting Goldy another calculating look. "Not a soul."

Two more patrol cars pulled to a stop in the middle of the street, behind and ahead of them. Four cops hit the pavement running, but the cops questioning the occupants of the taxi waved them off. They turned, undecided, ran back to their patrol cars, roared off toward the dark parking lot beside the Polo Grounds.

"Where are you folks going?" the cop asked Goldy.

Goldy crossed his index fingers over the gold cross at his bosom and said piously, "To heaven, bless the Lord, have mercy on our souls."

The cops thought he was performing some cabalistic ritual and hesitated. But Goldy had seen the young colored driver look half around, then turn back and look rigidly ahead. He could feel Slim trembling in the seat beside him. He was trying desperately to stall the cops and at the same time prevent Slim from repeating the lie about taking Imabelle to the hospital, because even one look at Imabelle was enough to tell she was healthy as a breeding mare.

"Maybe they went that way," he added before the cops could repeat the question, and made two circles with the gold cross.

The cops stared in fascination. They'd seen many strange religious sects in Harlem, and they respected the colored folks' religion on orders from the Commissioner. But this nun looked as though she might be worshipping the devil.

Finally one of the cops replied seriously, "What way?"

"The way of the transgressor is hard," Goldy said.

The cops exchanged glances.

"Let's get on," the first cop said.

The second cop gave Slim and Imabelle another scrutinizing look. "Are these folks disciples of yours, Sister?" he asked.

Suddenly Goldy put the gold cross into his mouth, then spat it out.

" 'And I took the little book out of the angel's hand, and ate it up,' " he quoted enigmatically. He knew the best way to confuse a white cop in Harlem was to quote foolishly from the Bible.

The cops' eyes stretched. Their cheeks puffed and their faces reddened as they tried to control their laughter. They touched their caps respectfully and turned quickly away. They were confused, but not suspicious.

"You think she's drunk?" one asked, loud enough for them to hear.

The other shrugged. "Either that or hopped."

They went back to their patrol car, made a screaming U-turn, and roared off toward the jungle of piers beneath the bridge.

Already people were collecting, emerging from the darkness like half-dressed phantoms.

The taxi started up again. The driver eased it cautiously past the patrol cars.

"Mother-raper, step on it!" Slim snarled.

The driver didn't relax the rigid set of his head but the taxi picked up speed and went fast down Eighth Avenue. Even the back of the driver's head looked scared.

"God damn it, get off me," Slim cursed, pushing Imabelle aside. "I'm burning up."

"Don't talk to me like that," she said, fumbling in her pocketbook.

"If you draw a knife on me—" Slim began, but she cut him off. "Shut up." She handed him a jar of face cream. "Here, put some of this on your burn."

He unscrewed the cap and smeared the white cream thickly over his acid burns.

"Hank shouldn't have done that," Imabelle said.

"Shut up yourself!" Slim grated. "Don't you know this old nun's a stool pigeon?"

Goldy felt Imabelle looking at him curiously, and bowed his head over the gold cross as though absorbed in devout meditation.

"You suspect everybody," Imabelle said to Slim. "How is she going to know what we talking about?"

"If you keep on talking you gonna make me have to cut her throat."

"All of you is knife-happy."

"Woe is past," Goldy said prayerfully.

"It's a good thing she's hopped," Slim muttered.

An ambulance came screaming up the street.

No one spoke again until they reached Kinckerbocker Hospital. Slim stopped the taxi in front of the main entrance instead of having it circle the ramp to the emergency entrance. He followed Imabelle out and took her by the arm and hurried her up the stairs without stopping to pay the fare.

Goldy ordered the driver to circle the block. When they came back Slim and Imabelle were getting into a taxi ahead.

Goldy ordered his driver to follow them. The driver grumbled.

"I hope us ain't getting in no trouble, ma'am."

" 'There were four and twenty elders,' " Goldy quoted, giving the driver a prediction for the day's number.

He knew that most folks in Harlem believed that holy people could look straight up into heaven and find the number coming out that day any time they wished.

The driver got the idea. He twisted his head and gave the nun a toothy grin. "Yas'm, four and twenty olders. Which one of them olders going to get here first, you reckon?"

"Four of the elders will lead the twenty," Goldy said.

"Yas'm."

The driver resolved to put five bucks on four twenty in each of Harlem's four big books before noon that day as sure as his name was Beau Diddley.

They followed the taxi of Slim and Imabelle until it stopped before a dark cold-water tenement on Upper Park Avenue. But they'd stuck so close they had to go on past when the taxi stopped. Goldy crouched out of sight in the back seat. He knew they hadn't got hep to his trailing them because they hadn't tried to lose him, but he wasn't sure whether they had recognized the taxi when it passed or not. It was a chance he had to take.

By the time they'd circled the block again, the other taxi was gone. Goldy watched the front of the tenement building, wondering whether he'd have to go inside and search for the flat.

But after a moment a light showed briefly in a front window on the third floor before the curtain was pulled. He was satisfied with that. He had the driver take him to the tobacco store on 121st Street.

Jackson was nowhere in sight. Goldy began to worry. He let himself into the store, went back to his room, lit the kerosene stove and cooked a C and M speedball over his alcohol lamp.

He had told Jackson to return there in case there was a rumble. But he had no way of knowing whether Jackson was dead or alive. And it was too early to ask at the precinct station. If anything had happened to either Grave Digger or Coffin Ed, the white cops might get suspicious and dig him too.

When the dope started working on his imagination, he could see everybody dead. He banged himself again to calm his fears.

94

CHAPTER 14

WHEN JACKSON emerged from the narrow passageway, a crowd had already collected in the street. He looked like something the Harlem River had spewed up. His overcoat was torn, the buttons missing, the sleeve slashed, he was covered with black muck, dripping dirty slime; his mouth was swollen, his eyes were red, and he looked half dead.

But the other people didn't look much better. The sound of pistol shooting and the screaming of the patrol car sirens had brought them rushing from their beds to see the cause of the excitement. It sounded like a battle royal taking place, and shootings and cuttings and folks dead and dying were a big show in Harlem.

Men, women and children had piled into the street, wrapped in blankets, two and three overcoats, pyjama legs showing over the tops of rubber overshoes, towels tied about their heads, draped with dusty rugs snatched hastily from the floor. Alongside some of the apparitions, Jackson looked like a man of elegance.

Most of them were milling about the police cordon that blocked the entrance to the alleyway on the other side of the Heaven, leading back to the shack where the shooting had taken place. Necks were craned, people stood on tiptoe, some sat astride others' backs trying to see what was happening.

Only one man wrapped up in a dirty yellow blanket like a black cocoon saw Jackson slip from the hole. Two cops were approaching, so all he did was wink.

The cops were looking at Jackson suspiciously and preparing to question him when a fist fight broke out among

95

the crowd on the other side. They hurried to join the group of harness cops converging on the fighters.

Jackson followed quickly, squeezed into the crowd.

"Let them niggers fight," he heard somebody say.

"Start one fight and everybody wanna fight," someone else said.

"Everybody in Harlem's a two-gun badman anyway. All they need is some horses and some cows and they'd all be rustlers."

Jackson couldn't see the fighters, but he kept worming toward the center of the crowd, trying to get lost.

A man looked at him and said, "This joker's been fighting too. Who you been fighting, shorty, yo' old lady?"

Somebody laughed.

Jackson noticed a cop looking at him. He started moving in another direction.

"They done croaked a copper," a voice said. "That's what they done."

The mob rolled back toward the cordon. The fist fight seemed to have been quelled.

"White copper?"

"Yeah, man."

"They gonna be some ass flying every whichway in Harlem 'fore this night's over."

"You ain't just saying it."

Jackson had wormed to the edge of the crowd and found himself face to face with the two cops who'd first noticed him.

"Hey, you!" one of them called.

He ducked back into the crowd. The cops started plowing after him.

Suddenly the attention of the crowd was attracted by the sound of enraged dogs growling. It sounded like a pack of wolves battling over a carcass.

"Hey, man, look at dis!" someone yelled.

The mob surged in a solid mass toward the sound of fighting dogs, sweeping Jackson away from the pursuing cops.

On the other side of the Heaven, directly in front of the

passage where Jackson had escaped, two huge dogs were rolling, snapping, growling, and slavering in a furious fight. One was a Doberman Pinscher the size of a grandfather wolf; the other a Great Dane as big as a Shetland pony. They belonged to two pimps who had been walking them at the time the shooting broke out. The pimps had to walk them two or three times every night because the flats they lived in were so small they had to keep the dogs chained up all the time, and the dogs howled and kept them awake. They'd taken them off the chains to let them run. The dogs were so vicious they'd started fighting on sight.

They rolled back and forth across the sidewalk, into the gutter and out again, fangs flashing in the dim light like mouths full of knives. The pimps were flailing the fighting dogs with their iron chains. Others scattered when the dogs rolled near.

"I got five bones says the black dog wins by a knockout," a man said.

"Who you kidding?" another man replied. "I takes a black dog any day in the year."

The cops neglected Jackson momentarily to separate the dogs. They approached cautiously with drawn pistols.

"Don't shoot my dog, mister," one of the pimps pleaded.

"They ain't gonna hurt nobody," the other pimp added.

The cops hesitated.

"Why aren't those dogs muzzled?" one of the cops asked.

"They was muzzled," the pimp lied. "They lost their muzzles fighting."

"Only way you can separate them is with fire," an onlooker said.

"Them dogs needs shooting," someone replied.

"Who's got some newspaper?" the first pimp asked.

Someone ran to get some newspaper from a junk cart parked at the curb up the street. It was a dilapidated wagon with cardboard sides and bowlegged wheels pulled by a mangy, purblind, splay-legged horse that would never eat grass again. The junkman who owned it had joined the crowd around the fighting dogs.

A man grabbed a piece of newspaper from the stack

97

the junkman had collected, brought it back on the run. He rumpled it into a torch and someone set it on fire and threw it beneath the fighting dogs. In the brief light supplied by the blaze the Doberman's bared fangs could be seen sinking into the Great Dane's throat.

The policeman leaned over and clubbed the Doberman on the head with the butt of his pistol.

"Don't kill my dog," the pimp whined.

Jackson saw the cart and headed toward it, climbed up into the seat, took the frayed rope reins and said, "Giddap."

The horse stretched its scabby neck and twisted its head about to look at Jackson. The horse didn't know the voice. But he couldn't see as far as Jackson.

"Giddap," Jackson said again and lashed the horse's flanks with the rope reins.

The horse straightened out its neck and started moving. But it moved in slow motion, like a motion picture slowed down, its legs moving with each step as though floating slowly through the air.

A cop Jackson hadn't seen before appeared suddenly and stopped him.

"Have you been here all the time?"

"Nawsuh. Ah just driv up," Jackson said, speaking in dialect to impress the cop that was the rightful junkman.

The cop had no doubts about Jackson being a junkman. He just wanted information.

"And you didn't see anyone running past you who looked suspicious?"

"He just driv up," the man said who had seen Jackson emerging from between the buildings. "Ah seed him."

It was the code of Harlem for one brother to help another lie to white cops.

"I didn't ask you," the cop said.

"Ah ain't seed nobody," Jackson said. "Ah just setting here minding my own business and ain't seed nobody."

"Who hit you in the mouth?"

"Two young boys tried to rob me. But dat was right after dark."

The cop was irritated. Questioning colored people always irritated that cop.

"Let's see your license," he demanded.

"Yassuh." Jackson began fumbling in his coat pockets, going from one to another. "Ah got it right heah."

A police sergeant shouted to the cop.

"What are you doing with that man?"

"Just questioning him."

The sergeant looked briefly at Jackson.

"Let him go. Come here and help block this entrance." He pointed to the passage through which Jackson had escaped. "We have a man corned back there somewhere and he might try to come through here."

"Yes, sir." The cop went to block the exit.

Jackson's colored friend winked at him.

"De hoss is gone, ain't he?"

Jackson exchanged looks. He couldn't take a chance on winking.

"Giddap," he said to the nag, beating its flanks with the reins.

The nag moved off in slow motion, impervious to Jackson's blows. At that moment the junkman looked from the crowd to see if his property was safe and saw Jackson driving off in his cart. He looked at Jackson as though he didn't believe it.

"Man, dass my wagon."

He was an old man dressed in cast-off rags and a horse blanket worn like a shawl. He had a black woolen cloth wrapped about his head like a turban, over which was pulled a floppy, stained hat. Kinky white hair sprouting from beneath the turban joined a kinky white beard, grimy with dirt and stained with tobacco juice, from which peered a wrinkled black face and watery old eyes. His shoes were wrapped in gunny sacks tied with string. He looked like Uncle Tom, down and out in Harlem.

"Hey!" he yelled at Jackson in a high, whining voice. "You stealin' mah wagon."

Jackson lashed the nag's rump, trying to get away. The junkman ran after him in a shuffling gait. Both horse and man moved so slowly it seemed to Jackson as though the whole world had slowed down to a crawl.

"Hey, he stealin' mah wagon."

A cop looked around at Jackson.

"Are you stealing this man's wagon?"

"Nawsuh, dat's mah pa. He can't see well."

The junkman clutched the cop's sleeve.

"Ah ain't you pa and Ah sees enough to see that you is stealing my wagon."

"Pa, you drunk," Jackson said.

The cop bent down and smelled the junkman's breath. He drew back quickly, blowing. "Whew."

"Come on and git in, Pa," Jackson said, winking at the junkman over the cop's head.

The junkman knew the code. Jackson was trying to get away and he wasn't going to be the one to rat on him to a white cop.

"Ah din see dat was you, son," he said, climbing up onto the seat beside Jackson.

The cop shrugged and turned away disgustedly.

The junkman fished a dirty plug of chewing tobacco from his coat pocket, blew the trash from it, bit off a chew, and offered it to Jackson. Jackson declined. The junkman stuck the plug back into his pocket, picked up the rope reins, shook them gently and whined, "Giddyap, Jebusite."

Jebusite drifted off as though coasting through space. The junkman reined him between the score of patrol cars parked at all angles in the street like tanks stalled in a desert.

Farther down the street civilian cars were parked, others were coming, curious people were converging from every direction. The word that a white cop had been killed had hit the neighborhood like a stroke of lightning.

The junkman didn't say anything until they were five blocks away. Then he asked, "Did you done it?"

"Done what?"

"Croaked dat cop?"

"I ain't done nothing."

"Den what you runnin' for?"

"I just don't want to get caught."

The junkman understood. Colored folks in Harlem didn't want to get caught by the police whether they had done anything or not.

"Me neither," he said.

He spat a stream of tobacco juice into the street and wiped his mouth with the back of his dirty cotton glove.

"You got a bone?"

Jackson started to take out his roll, thought better of it, skinned off a dollar bill and handed it to the junkman.

The junkman looked at it carefully and then tucked it out of sight beneath his rags. At 142nd Street, directly in front of the house where Jackson and Imabelle had formerly roomed, he stopped the horse, got out and started picking over the pile of garbage.

Jackson thought of Imabelle for the first time since he'd begun his escape. His heart came up and spread out in his mouth.

"Hey," he called. "You want to take me down to 121st Street?"

The junkman looked up with an armful of trash.

"You got another bone?"

Jackson skinned off another dollar bill. The junkman threw the trash into the back of the wagon, climbed back to his seat, stashed the dollar and shook the reins. The nag floated off.

They rode in silence.

Jackson felt as though he were at the bottom of the pit. He'd been clubbed, cut at, shot at, skinned up, chased, and humiliated. The knot on his head sent pain shooting down through his skull like John Henry driving steel, and his puffed, bruised lips throbbed like tom-toms.

He didn't know whether Goldy had found Imabelle's address, whether she'd been arrested, whether she was dead or alive. He hardly knew how he'd gotten out alive himself, but that didn't matter. He was sitting there riding in a junk wagon and he didn't know anything. For all he knew, right at that moment, his woman might be in deadly danger. What was more, now that the gang knew the police were on to them, they might run away with Imabelle's gold ore. But just so long as they didn't hurt Imabelle, he didn't care.

His clothes were wet on the outside from the puddle he'd fallen into, and wet on the inside from his own pure sweat. And all of it was icy cold. He sat trembling from cold and worry, and couldn't do a thing.

Colored people passed along the dark sidewalks, slinking cautiously past the dark, dangerous doorways, heads bowed, every mother's child of them looking as though they had trouble.

Colored folks and trouble, Jackson thought, like two mules hitched to the same wagon.

"You cold?" the junkman asked.

"I ain't warm."

"Wanna drink?"

"Where's it at?"

The junkman fished a bottle of smoke from his ragged garments.

"You got another bone?"

Jackson skinned off another dollar bill, handed it to the junkman, took the bottle and tilted it to his lips. His teeth chattered on the bottle neck. The smoke burnt his gullet and simmered in his belly, but it didn't make him feel any better.

He handed the half-emptied bottle back.

"You got a woman?" the junkman asked.

"I got one," Jackson said mournfully. "But I don't know where she's at."

The junkman looked at Jackson, looked at the bottle of smoke, handed it back to Jackson.

"You keep it," he said. "You need it more'n me."

CHAPTER 15

GOLDY was standing in the dark, watching through the glass front door of the tobacco shop, when Jackson got down from the junk wagon. He opened the door for Jackson to enter, and locked it behind him.

"Did you find out where she's at?" Jackson asked immediately.

"Come on back to my room where we can talk."

"Talk? What for?"

"Be quiet, man."

They groped through the black dark like two ghosts, invisible to each other. Jackson begrudged every second wasted. Goldy was trying to figure out where to hide the gold ore when he'd finally gotten it.

Goldy turned on the light in his room and padlocked the door on the inside.

"What you locking the door for?" Jackson complained. "Ain't you found out where she's at?"

Before replying, Goldy went around the table and sat down. His wig and bonnet lay on the table beside a half-empty bottle of whiskey. With his round black head poking from the bulging black gown, he looked like an African sculpture. He was so high he kept brushing imaginary specks from his gown.

"I found out where she's at all right, but first I got to know what happened."

Jackson stood just inside the door. He began swelling with rage. "Goldy, unlock this door. I feel like I'm just two feet away from jail as it is."

103

Goldy got up to unlock the door, shoulders twitching from the gage.

"Aw, God damn it, set down and cool off," he muttered. "Drink some of that whiskey there. You're making me nervous."

Jackson drank from the bottle. His teeth chattered so loudly on the bottle neck that Goldy jumped.

"Man, quit making those sudden noises. You sound like a rattlesnake."

Jackson banged the bottle on the table and gave Goldy a look of blue violence.

"Be careful, Brother, be careful. I've taken all I'm going to take this night from anybody. You just tell me where my woman is and I'll go get her."

Goldy sat down again and began shining his cross with quick, jerky motions. "You tell me first what happened."

"You ought to know what happened if you found out where she's at."

"Listen, man, we're just wasting time like this. I wasn't back there when the rumble happened. I was setting in a taxi out front when she and Slim came out and got in and he said she was his wife and had taken poison and he had to get her to Knickerbocker Hospital. They rode with me to the hospital then got out and switched taxis and rode over to the place on Park Avenue where they stay. I followed them and that's all I know. Now you tell me what happened back there in the shack so we can figure out what to do."

Jackson began to worry again.

"Do they know you followed them?"

"How do I know? Slim don't know, anyway, unless Imabelle told him. He was in too much pain to notice anything."

"Did some get in his eyes too?"

"Naw, just on his neck and face."

"Did they act suspicious of you?"

"I don't know. Quit asking so many questions and just tell me what you know."

"What I know don't matter if they know you followed

104

them. Because by this time Slim will be long gone from wherever he's at, if he's still got his sight."

"Listen, Bruzz," Goldy said, trying to remain patient. "That woman is sharp. Chances are that she knows I followed her. But that don't mean she tells Slim. That depends on how she's playing it. One thing is sure, she has turned you in for a new model. That's for sure."

"I know she ain't done that," Jackson insisted doggedly.

"No you don't neither, Bruzz. But whether she's ready to turn Slim in now for another new model, nobody can say."

"That just ain't so."

"All right, square. Have it whatever way you wish. We're going to find out soon enough if you ever get around to telling me what happened back there."

"Well, Grave Digger shot Gus through the head, and Hank threw acid into Coffin Ed's eyes—that's when it got on Slim. Then the lights went out and there was a lot of shooting and fighting in the dark. Somebody was trying to cut Imabelle. I got knocked out trying to get to her to help her. And by the time I came to everybody was gone."

"Holy jumping Joseph! Did Grave Digger get killed too?"

"I don't know. When I came to he was lying on the floor —leastways I think it was him—and there weren't anybody left but me and Coffin Ed. And he was going crazy with pain, in there blind, with a loaded pistol, ready to shoot anything that moved. Only the Lord in Heaven knows how I got out of there alive."

Goldy got up abruptly and put on his wig and bonnet. Suddenly he was consumed with haste.

"Listen, we got to work fast now because those studs is hotter here in Harlem than a down-home coke oven."

"That's what I've been saying all along. Let's go."

Goldy paused long enough to give him an angry look.

"Man, wait a minute, God damn it. We can't go in our bare asses."

He raised the mattress of the couch and took out a big blued-steel Frontier Colt's .45 six-shooter.

"Great day alive! You had that thing in here all along!" Jackson exclaimed.

"You just look over there in that corner and get that piece of pipe and don't ask so many questions."

Jackson felt in behind the stack of cardboard cartons and hauled out a three-foot length of one-inch iron pipe. One end was wrapped with black machinist's tape to form a hand hold. He hoisted it once to get the feel but didn't say anything.

Goldy slipped the .45 revolver into the folds of his Sister of Mercy gown. Jackson stuck the homemade bludgeon beneath his wet, tattered overcoat. Goldy turned out the light and padlocked the door. They moved through the blackness of the store toward the front door, like two ghosts armed for mayhem.

It was snowing slightly when they got outside. The white snowflakes turned a dirty gray when they hit the black street.

"We got to get some way to move her trunk," Goldy said.

A black cat slunk from beneath a wet crate filled with garbage. Goldy kicked at it viciously.

Jackson looked disapproving.

"Let's get one of those big DeSoto taxicabs."

"Man, quit thinking with your feet. That gold ore is hot enough by now to burn a hole through the Harlem River."

"Maybe we can find that junk wagon I came home in."

"That ain't the lick either. What you got to do is steal your boss's hearse."

Jackson stopped dead still to look at Goldy.

"Steal his hearse! She ain't dead, is she?"

"Jesus Christ, man, you going to be a square all your life. Naw, she ain't dead. But we gotta have some way to move the trunk."

"You want me to steal Mr. Clay's hearse to move the trunk in?"

"You done stole everything else by now, so what are you gagging on a hearse for? You already got the keys."

Jackson felt his pants-pocket. Attached to an iron chain

106

from his belt were the keys to both the pickup hearse and the garage where it was kept.

"You've been searching my pockets while I was asleep."

"What difference does it make? You ain't got nothing for nobody to steal. Come on, let's go."

Silently they trudged up Seventh Avenue.

Most of the bars were closed. But people were still in the street, heads drawn down into turned-up collars beneath pulled-down hats, like headless people. They came and went from the apartment houses where the after-hours joints were jumping and the house-rent parties swimming and the whores plying their trade and the gamblers clipping chumps.

Traffic still rolled along the avenue, trucks and buses headed north, across the 155th Street Bridge and on up the Saw Mill River Parkway to Westchester County and beyond. Cars and taxis rushed past, stopped short, people got in and out, the cars stayed put and the taxis went on again.

Red-eyed patrol cars darted about like angry bugs, screaming to a stop, cops hitting flatfooted on the pavement, picking up every suspicious-looking character for the lineup. A black hoodlum had thrown acid in a black detective's eyes and black asses were going to pay for it as long as black asses lasted.

Masquerading as Sister Gabriel, Goldy trudged along the slushy street like a tired saint, holding the gold cross before him like a shield, scrunching to one side to hide the bulging bulk of the Western .45.

Jackson walked beside him, hugging the length of pipe beneath his dirty coat.

A half-high miss coming from an after-hours joint looked at them and said to her tall, dark escort, "He look just like her brother, don't he?"

"Short, black, and squatty," the tall man said.

"Hush! Don't talk such way 'bout a nun."

No police stopped them, nobody molested them. Goldy's black gown and gold cross covered them with safety.

The garage was on the same street as the funeral parlor, half a block distant. When they came to 133rd Street they turned over to Lenox Avenue and came back on 134th Street to keep from being seen.

Jackson unlocked the door and led the way inside. "Shut the door," he said to Goldy as he groped for the light-switch.

"What for, man? You don't need no light. Just get in the wagon and back it out."

"I got to change clothes. I'm freezing to death in these."

"Man, you got more excuses than Lazarus," Goldy complained, closing the door. "We ain't got all night."

"It ain't you that's freezing," Jackson said angrily as he stripped to his long damp drawers, stained black from the dye of his suit, put on an old dark gray uniform and overcoat that hung on a nail, and his new chauffeur's cap he took from a tool chest.

When he turned to climb into the driver's seat he noticed that the back of the hearse was loaded with funeral paraphernalia. It was a 1947 Cadillac that had first seen service as an ambulance. Now it was used mainly to pick up the bodies for embalming, and to do double duty as a truck. The coffin rack was half hidden beneath a pile of black bunting used to drape the rostrum during a funeral, plaster pedestals for lights and flowers, wreaths of artificial flowers, and a bucket half-filled with dirty motor-oil changed from one of the limousines.

Jackson opened the back double-doors, took out the motor-oil, and started to unload the other things.

"Leave that junk be," Goldy said. "All the time you're taking a man would think you don't care what happens to your old lady."

"I want to hurry more than you," Jackson defended himself. "I was just trying to make space for the trunk."

"We'll put it where they put the coffins. Come on, man, let's hurry."

Jackson slammed shut the back doors, went around to the front and got behind the wheel. He turned on the switch, read the gauges from habit, told Goldy to turn out the light and open the door. He started the motor and backed into the street, straight into the path of a patrol car.

The cop driving stopped the car. They looked from the nun to the driver, and alighted very deliberately, one from one side, one from the other. Moving with the same deliberation, Goldy closed and locked the garage door, thinking fast. He decided they were just meddling; he had to chance it, anyway. He walked back to meet the cops, touching his gold cross.

Jackson looked at the cops and felt the sweat dripping from his face onto his hands, running down his neck.

"Are you riding with this hearse, Sister?" one of the cops asked, touching his cap respectfully.

"Yes, sir, in the service of the Lord," Goldy said slowly in his most prayerful-sounding voice. "To take that which is left of him who hath been taken in the first death, praise the Lord, to wait in the endless river until he shall be taken in the second death."

Both cops looked at Goldy uncomprehendingly.

"You mean to pick up a dead body."

"Yes, sir, to gather in the remains of him who hath been taken in the first death."

The cops exchanged glances. The other one walked up to Jackson and flashed his light into Jackson's face. Jackson's wet face glistened like a smooth wet lump of coal. The cop bent down to smell his breath.

"This driver looks drunk. I can smell the whiskey on him."

"No sir, I'm not drunk," Jackson denied. He merely looked scared, but the cop didn't know it. "I had a drink but I ain't drunk."

"Get out," the cop ordered.

Jackson got out, moving as carefully with the pipe hidden beneath his coat as though his bones were made of sugar candy.

"Walk in a straight line to that post," the cop ordered, pointing to a lamp post on the other side of the street.

To distract the cops' attention, Goldy quoted huskily, " 'And he laid hold on the dragon—' "

The cops turned to look at him.

"What's that, Sister?"

" 'That old serpent,' " Goldy quoted, " 'which is the Devil, and Satan, and bound him a thousand years.' "

By that time Jackson had gotten to the post. But Goldy's dodge had been unnecessary. In order to keep the pipe from slipping from beneath his coat, Jackson had walked as rigidly as a zombie and as straight as the path of a bullet. But sweat was running down his legs.

"He looks sober enough," the first cop said.

"Yeah, he seems steady enough," the second cop agreed.

Neither one of them had watched him walking.

"Get back in, boy, and take this nun on her errand of mercy."

"It's mighty late to be picking up a body at this hour," the second cop remarked.

"Nobody can choose their time to go to the first death," Goldy replied. "They go when the wagon of the Lord calls for them, early or late."

The cop smiled. "We all got to go when the wagon comes. Isn't that what they say here in Harlem?"

"Yes, sir, the wagon of the Lord."

"Whose body is it?"

"Nobody can claim it now," Goldy said. "We just take it and bury it."

The cops were tired of trying to get any sense out of the nun. They shrugged and got back into their patrol car and drove away.

CHAPTER 16

LOOKING eastward from the towers of Riverside Church, perched among the university buildings on the high banks of the Hudson River, in a valley far below, waves of gray rooftops distort the perspective like the surface of a sea. Below the surface, in the murky waters of fetid tenements, a city of black people who are convulsed in desperate living, like the voracious churning of millions of hungry cannibal fish. Blind mouths eating their own guts. Stick in a hand and draw back a nub.

That is Harlem.

The farther east it goes, the blacker it gets.

East of Seventh Avenue to the Harlem River is called The Valley. Tenements thick with teeming life spread in dismal squalor. Rats and cockroaches compete with the mangy dogs and cats for the man-gnawed bones.

The apartment where Slim and Imabelle lived was on Upper Park Avenue, between 129th and 130th Streets. That part of The Valley was called the Dusty Bottom of the Coal Bin.

The trestle of the New York Central railroad, coming from Grand Central out of ground at 95th Street and crossing overtop at the 125th Street Station, runs down the center of the street in place of the park in the downtown section from which the avenue derives its name.

It converges onto the trestle of the Third Avenue Elevated line, then curves across the Harlem River into the Bronx and the big wide world beyond.

Up there in Harlem, Park Avenue is flanked by cold-water, dingy tenement buildings, brooding between junk yards, dingy warehouses, factories, garages, trash-dumps where smart young punks raise marihuana weed.

It is a truck-rutted street of violence and danger, known in the underworld as the Bucket-of-Blood. See a man lying in the gutter, leave him lay, he might be dead.

The fat black men in their black garments in the creeping black hearse were part of the eerie night. The old Cadillac motor, in excellent repair, purred softly as a kitten. Snow floated vaguely through the dim lights.

"That's it," Goldy pointed out.

Jackson looked at a doorway to one side of the dirty broken plate-glass windows of a hide shop. A moth-eaten steer's head stared back at him through mismatched glass eyes. His skin sprouted goose pimples. He had come to the end of the trail and he was so scared he didn't know whether to be glad or sorry.

"Just park right here," Goldy said. "Makes no difference."

Jackson brought the hearse to a stop and doused the lights.

A truck rumbled past, headed downtown toward the Harlem Market beyond 116th Street, leaving a darker gloom in its wake.

He and Goldy peered up and down the deserted street. Jackson felt his flesh crawl.

"Can they see us?" he asked.

"Not if they ain't looking."

That wasn't what Jackson meant, but he didn't argue. He reached beneath his overcoat for his iron pipe.

"It's ain't time for your club yet," Goldy cautioned.

Jackson was reluctant to get out of the hearse.

"I'm going to leave the motor running," he said.

"What for? You want to get it stolen?"

"Nobody'd steal a hearse."

"What you talking about? These folks over here'll steal a blind man's eyes."

Goldy alighted to the sidewalk noiselessly. Jackson took a deep breath and followed. They went across the sidewalk, entered a long, narrow hall lit by a dim fly-specked bulb.

Graffiti decorated the whitewashed walls. Huge genitals hung from crude dwarfed torsos like a harvest of strange fruit. Someone had drawn a nude couple in a sex embrace. Others had added to it. Now it was a mural.

It was a long hall, diminishing into shadow. At the far end stairs climbed steeply into pitch darkness.

Goldy led the way, tiptoeing, the hem of his long black gown sweeping the dirty floor. He went noiselessly up the wooden stairs, disappeared so suddenly in the overhead dark that Jackson's scalp twitched. Jackson followed, his fat flesh running with ice cold sweat. He took out his pipe again and gripped the taped handle.

The dark hallways above smelled of stale urine and neglected dirt.

Goldy climbed to the third floor, went down the hall to the door at the front. When Jackson caught up he saw the dull blue gleam of Goldy's revolver in the dark.

Goldy knocked softly on the scabby brown door, once; then three times rapidly, once more, then twice rapidly.

"Is that the signal?" Jackson asked in a whisper.

"How the hell do I know?" Goldy whispered in reply.

Silence greeted them.

"Maybe they've left," Jackson whispered.

"We'll soon find out."

"Then what we going to do?"

Goldy gestured for silence, knocked again, softly, changing the signal.

"What are you doing that for if you don't know the signal?"

"I'm crossing 'em up."

"You think more than just Slim is here?"

"What the hell do I care? As long as the gold is here."

"Maybe they've taken it."

Goldy waited and knocked again, softly, giving another signal.

From behind the door a cautious voice asked, "Who there?" It sounded like the voice of a woman with her mouth held close to the panel.

Goldy poked Jackson in the ribs with the muzzle of his

113

revolver, signaling him to answer the voice. But it gave Jackson such a scare he bolted like a wild horse and his pipe flew out and hit the door with a bang that sounded like a gunshot in the pitch-black, silent hall.

"Who there?" a high feminine voice asked in panic.

"It's me, Jackson. Is that you, Imabelle?"

"Jackson!" the voice said in amazement. It sounded as though it had never heard of Jackson.

Silence reigned.

"It's me, honey. Your Jackson."

After a moment the voice asked suspiciously, "If you is Jackson what is the first name of your boss?"

"Hosea. Hosea Exodus Clay. You know that as well as me, honey."

"What a square," Goldy muttered to himself.

A lock was turned, then another, then a bolt was slipped back. The door opened a crack, held by an iron chain.

A dim droplight was burning in a squalid bedroom. Jackson stuck his shiny black face into the crack of light.

"Oh, sugar!" The chain was unhooked and the door flung open. "Lawd, is I glad to see you!"

Jackson had just time to see that she was dressed in a red dress and a black coat before she fell into his arms. She smelled like burnt hair-grease, hot-bodied woman, and dime-store perfume. Jackson embraced her, holding the iron pipe clutched against her spine. She wriggled against the curve of his fat stomach and welded her rouge-greasy mouth against his dry, puckered lips.

Then she drew back.

"Lawd, Daddy, I thought you'd never come."

"I came as soon as I could get here, honey."

She held him at arms' length, looked at the pipe still gripped in his hand, then looked at his face and read him like a book. She ran the tip of her red tongue slowly across her full, cushiony, sensuous lips, making them wetted, and looked him straight in the eyes with her own glassy, speckled bedroom-eyes.

The man drowned.

When he came up, he stared back, passion cocked, his

whole black being on a live-wire edge. Ready! Solid ready to cut throats, crack skulls, dodge police, steal hearses, drink muddy water, live in a hollow log, and take any rape-fiend chance to be once more in the arms of his high-yellow heart.

"Where's Slim? I'm going to bash that bastard's brains to a raspberry pulp, may the Lord forgive me," he said.

"He's gone. He just left. Come on inside, quick. He's coming back in a minute."

When Jackson stepped into the room, Goldy followed.

There was a battered white-painted iron double bed against one wall, with the covers turned back, exposing dirty stained sheets and two pillows with slimy gray circles from hair grease. Against the other wall was an over-stuffed sofa with the heads of two springs poking from the rotten faded green seat-covering. At the back a rusty potbellied stove squatted on a square of rusty tin. To one side was a wooden box serving as a coalbin, to the other a doorway leading into the kitchen. A round table with a knife-scarred top and a three-legged straight-backed chair commanded the center of the bare wooden floor. The room was filled to the brim. When the three people entered, it overflowed.

"What's she doing here?" Imabelle asked, throwing a startled look at Goldy.

"He's my brother. He's come to help me get you away."

She looked at the big .45 in Goldy's hand. Her eyes stretched and her lips twitched. But she didn't look surprised.

"You-all has sure come loaded for bear."

"Can't come as boys to do a man's job," Goldy said.

She peered at Goldy.

"He sure looks like that Sister me and Slim rode with."

"I is." Goldy grinned, showing his two gold teeth. "That's how I found out where you is at. I trailed you."

"Well, how 'bout that! Impersonating a nun. Everybody got their racket, ain't they?"

Goldy saw the trunk first. It was at the end of the sofa, hidden from Jackson's view by the table.

"What they been doing to you, honey?" Jackson asked anxiously.

Suddenly Imabelle got into a lather of haste.

"Daddy, we ain't got time to talk. Slim has gone after Hank and Jodie. They're coming back to take my gold ore. You got to save my gold ore, Daddy."

"What else am I here for, honey? Just tell me where it's at."

He was looking through the doorway into the kitchen. The only clean thing in that flat was the kitchen floor. It was still wet from a recent scrubbing.

"It ain't in there," Goldy said, pointing toward the trunk.

"Daddy, is I glad you come!" Imabelle repeated in a loud voice, and went around the table to get her pocketbook from beneath a pillow.

"Don't you worry, I'll save your gold, honey. I brought the hearse."

"The hearse! Mr. Clay's hearse?"

She went to the front window and peeked through the drawn shades. When she turned back she was giggling.

"Well, how 'bout that!"

"Only thing we could get to move it with," Jackson said defensively.

"Let's just take it and go, Daddy. I'll tell you everything on the way."

"Those bastards haven't hurt you, have they?"

"No, Daddy, but we ain't got time to talk about it now. We got to think of some place to hide the trunk at. They'll be looking for it everywhere."

"We can't take it home," Jackson said. "The landlady has put us out."

"We'll keep it in my room," Goldy said. "I got a room where nobody can find it. Bruzz'll tell you. It'll be safe there, won't it, Bruzz?"

"I'll think of some place," Jackson said evasively.

He had no intention of letting Goldy get his hands on that trunk full of gold ore.

"What's the matter with my place?"

"We ain't got time to argue," Imabelle said. "Slim'll be back any minute with Hank and Jodie."

"Ain't no argument," Goldy argued. "I has already got the best place."

"We'll check it at the station," Imabelle said as the thought struck her. "But for God's sake hurry up. We ain't got no time to lose."

Jackson stuck his pipe underneath his arm and circled the table to get to the trunk.

Goldy stuck his big .45 inside of his rusty black gown and gave Jackson a regretful look.

"The older you gets the more squared you becomes, Bruzz," he said sorrowfully.

Imabelle looked from one to another and came to a sudden decision. "Take it to your brother's place, Daddy. It'll be safe there."

Goldy and Imabelle exchanged glances.

"I'll wait for you-all in the hearse," she said.

"We're coming right after you," Jackson said, hoisting his end of the trunk.

Goldy hoisted the other end. They staggered beneath its weight, squeezed between the table and sofa, pushing the table aside, angled it through the narrow doorway.

They heard Imabelle's high heels tapping quickly down the wooden stairs.

"You go first," Goldy said.

Jackson turned his back to the trunk, took the bottom corners in each hand, let the weight rest on his back, led down the steep stairs, his legs buckling at every step.

He had sweated through the back of his coat by the time they came out onto the sidewalk. Sweat was running into his eyes, blinding him. He felt his way across the sidewalk to the back of the hearse, balanced the trunk with one hand, opened the double-doors with the other, moved some of the junk out of the way, and hoisted his end onto the coffin rack. Then he got back and helped Goldy push the trunk inside.

The trunk sat between the two side windows in clear view, like a sawed-off casket fitted to a legless man.

117

Jackson closed the doors and went around one side of the hearse to the driver's seat. Goldy went around the other. They looked at each other across the empty seat.

"Where'd she go?" Jackson asked.

"How the hell do I know where she went? She's your woman, she ain't mine."

Jackson peered up and down the dismal street. Far down on the other side, almost to the station, he saw some people running. It didn't attract his attention. Somebody was always running in Harlem.

"She must be somewheres."

Goldy climbed into the front seat, trying to be patient.

"Leave us take the trunk on home and come back for her."

"I can't leave her here. You know that. It was her I came after in the first place."

Goldy began losing his patience. "Man, let's go. That woman can find her way."

"You leave me run my own business," Jackson said, starting back into the tenement.

"She's not in the house, God damn it. Are you going to be a square all your life? She's gone."

"If she's gone I'm going to wait right here until she comes back."

Goldy was fingering the handle of his revolver as he struggled to control his fury.

"Man, all that bitch wants is to save her gold. She's going to find you. She don't care nothing 'bout nobody."

"I'm getting good and sick and tired of you talking about her like that," Jackson flared, approaching Goldy belligerently.

Goldy drew his revolver halfway out. It was all he could do to stop himself.

"God damn, you black son of a bitch, if you wasn't my brother I'd kill you," he said, twitching all over in a doped rage.

Jackson took a new grip on his length of iron pipe, crossed the sidewalk, climbed the tenement stairs back to the flat.

118

"Imabelle. You here, Imabelle?"

He searched the apartment, looking underneath the bed, behind the sofa, in the kitchen, holding the club gripped firmly in his hand, as though he were searching for someone as small as a puppy dog and dangerous as a male gorilla.

A corner of the kitchen was closed off with a faded green cotton curtain suspended from a line of sagging twine. Jackson pulled the curtain aside and looked inside.

"She left all her clothes," he said aloud.

Suddenly he felt beat, tired to the bone.

He sat down in the one kitchen chair, laid his head in the cushion of his folded arms on the kitchen table, closed his eyes in weariness, and the next instant he was asleep.

CHAPTER 17

A BLACK delivery truck made a fast turn into Park Avenue from 130th Street, heading south opposite the tenement building, and suddenly slackened speed.

From the driver's seat Jodie peered intently at the parked hearse. "There's a hearse out front," he said needlessly.

"I see it," Hank said, leaning forward to peer around his shoulder.

"What's it doing there, you reckon?"

"I ain't no fortuneteller."

"You reckon the cops are with it?"

"I don't reckon nothing. Let's find out."

Both of them had changed clothes since their escape from the shack on the Harlem River.

Jodie now wore a blue overcoat, black snap-brim hat parked on the back of his head, a blue suit, brown suede gloves, and black oxfords. He could have passed for a dining-car waiter, a job at which he'd been employed for four years.

Hank wore a dark brown overcoat, brown hat, and a blue suit. He had his hat pulled low over his eyes and both hands dug into his overcoat pockets.

They were dressed for a getaway.

From where he sat on the front seat of the hearse, Goldy saw the lights of the truck when it first turned into Park Avenue. When it turned so that he could see what type of truck it was, he was instantly suspicious. He knew that a delivery truck of that type had no business on that

120

kind of street at that time of night. He bent over on the seat so that he couldn't be seen, cocking his ears to listen. He heard the truck going slowly down the opposite side of the street. It occurred to him suddenly that it might be Hank and Jodie returning to get the trunk of gold ore. He took the revolver from the folds of his gown, held it against his chest, and twisted about on the seat so that he could see into the rear-view mirror.

When the panel truck was directly opposite the hearse, Jodie said, "It's empty."

"Looks empty."

"But there's something in the back. Reckon it's a coffin?"

"You do your own reckoning."

Suddenly Jodie could see past the end of the trunk through the opposite window.

"It ain't no coffin."

Hank took a .38 automatic from his right overcoat pocket and jacked a shell into the breech.

Jodie made a U-turn before reaching the end of the block, came back on the side of the hearse, then turned inside the iron stanchions of the trestle to pass it.

Goldy watched the lights in the rear-view mirror until they had passed out of range, but he heard the truck going slowly ahead.

Now Hank was on the inside of the truck, next to the hearse.

"There's a trunk in it," he said.

Jodie peered around Hank's shoulder.

"You reckon it's her trunk?"

"We're going to see."

Jodie steered the truck to the curb ahead of the hearse, parked, and doused the lights. He took off his gloves, put them into his left overcoat pocket, stuck his hand into his right pocket, and gripped the cold bone-handle of his knife.

He got out on the street side, while Hank alighted on the sidewalk. Both stood poised for an instant, casing the silent street. Then both turned in unison and walked back quietly

121

to the silent hearse. Both glanced casually into the front seat as they passed, but didn't notice Goldy. His black gown made him invisible in the dark.

At the sides of the hearse they stopped and peered through the glass windows, examining the trunk on the coffin rack. Their gazes met over the top. They went to the back of the hearse, tried the doors, found them open, and looked inside.

"It's it, all right," Jodie said.

"I can see it."

Goldy had raised his head slightly to watch them in the rear-view mirror. He recognized them instantly. From the way Hank stood with his right hand always in his pocket, Goldy knew he had a gun. He wasn't sure about Jodie, but he figured Hank was the one to watch.

He saw them turn and look up at the window of the third-floor flat.

"I don't see no light," Jodie said.

"That don't mean nothing."

"I'm gonna look."

"Wait a minute."

"I don't want to stand out here and get my ass blown off."

"If anybody's in there they've already seen us."

"What do you mean, if anybody's in there? You think spooks brought down this heavy trunk?"

"The way I figure it, she got Jackson to help her."

"Jackson. That mother-raping tarball. How the hell could he find out where she's at?"

"How the hell did he find out where our river hide-away was at? An eight-ball like him sweet on a high-yaller gal will find out where Hitler is buried at."

"Then it must be his boss's hearse."

"That's the way I figure it."

Jodie laughed softly.

"Let's take the mother-raping hearse too."

"Let's see if he left the keys in it."

When they turned back toward the front seat, Jodie on the street side and Hank on the sidewalk, Goldy felt along the sill of the street-side window and pushed down the button that locked the door. He figured that all Jodie had was a knife, and he could concentrate on Hank.

His body tensed as he watched their reflections vanish from the opposite edges of the rear-view mirror, his right arm stiffened, fingers tightened on the butt of the big .45. But he waited until Hank turned the handle of the front door before cocking the revolver in order to synchronize the sound with the clicking of the door lock.

Hank wasn't expecting danger from that source. When he pulled open the door, Goldy straightened up on the seat, looking like the mother of all the evil ghosts, and said, "Freeze!"

Hank looked into the muzzle of the .45 and froze. His heart stopped beating, his lungs stopped breathing, his blood stopped flowing. That big hole at the end of Goldy's .45 looked as big as a cannon bore.

Goldy figured he was protected from behind by the locked door. But the door locks on the old Cadillac hearse were out of order.

At the first sight of motion Jodie snatched open the door at Goldy's back with his left hand, snatched Goldy bodily from the seat into the street with his right hand before Goldy could squeeze the trigger, kicked the gun out of his hand while he was still in the air, kicked him again in the back of the neck the instant Goldy's fat black-gowned figure hit the pavement.

He didn't care whether it was a man, woman, or child he was kicking. He was riding a lightning bolt of maniacal violence, and all he could see was a red ball of murder.

As the revolver skidded down the street, he kicked Goldy in the ribs, and when the revolver bumped to a stop in the gutter against the curb and vanished in the black slush, he kicked Goldy in the back above the kidneys.

Hank was running around the front of the hearse with the cocked .38 automatic in his hand when Jodie kicked Goldy in the solar plexus.

"Leave off," Hank said, leveling the .38 on Jodie's heart. "You'll kill her."

Goldy writhed on the dirty wet bricks like a fish on a hook, gasping for breath. White froth had collected at the corners of his mouth before he could speak.

Jodie stood poised, anchored by Hank's gun, panting out his violence.

"One more kick and I'd a' killed her."

"Lawd, have mercy on an old lady," Goldy finally managed to wail.

The whistle of a train approaching the station sounded as it turned across the Harlem River like an echo to Goldy's wailing plea.

Hank stepped close to Goldy, suddenly reached down with his left hand and lifted Goldy's face by the chin.

Goldy was groping desperately for his gold cross that had got entangled in the folds of his gown.

"I'm a Sister of Mercy," he said in a moaning wail. "I'm in the service of the Lord."

"Don't hand us that crap, we know who you are," Hank said.

"She's that nun who stools for them two darky dicks ain't she? How you reckon she got in this deal?"

"How the hell do I know? Ask her."

Jodie looked down into Goldy's ash-gray face. There was no mercy in Jodie's muddy brown eyes.

"Talk fast," he said. " 'Cause you ain't got much time."

The sound of the approaching train, transmitted by the iron tracks on the iron trestle, slowly grew louder.

"Listen—" Goldy whined.

A short sharp blast of the train whistle, signaling that it had crossed the river into Harlem, cut him off.

"Listen, I can help you get away with it. You're strangers here, but I know this town in and out."

Hank's eyes narrowed. He was listening intently.

Jodie pulled his hand from his overcoat pocket, gripping the handle of his switch-blade knife. It had a push-button on the top of the handle, worked by the thumb, and when he pressed it a six-inch blade leaped forward with a soft click, gleaming dully in the dim light.

Goldy saw the blade from the corners of his eyes and scrambled to his knees.

"Listen, I can hide it for you."

His instinctive fear of cold steel made his eyes run tears.

"Listen, I can cover for you——"

Jodie showed his hatred for a stooly by slapping off Goldy's cap. The gray wig came off with it, leaving the round head exposed.

"This black mother-raper is a man," he said, moving around behind Goldy.

"Listen to him," Hank said.

"I got a hideout can't nobody find. Listen, I can take care of you-all. I can cover with the cops. I got ins at the precinct. You know my secret now. You know you can trust me. Listen, I can hide all of you, and there's enough for——" His voice was lost in the thunder of the approaching train.

Hank bent down to hear him better, staring into his face.

"Who else is with you?"

"Ain't nobody, I swear——"

The Diesel locomotive of the train was rumbling overhead. The trestle shook, shaking the stanchions. The street shook, the building shook, the whole black night was quaking.

Goldy knelt as though in prayer, knees planted on the wet, dirty-black shaking street, his fat body shaking beneath the flowing folds of the robe, shaking as though praying in a void of pure terror.

Jodie leaned forward quickly behind him. He was shaking too.

"Lying mother——," he said in a voice of rage.

Goldy realized instantly his mistake. Somebody had had to help him bring down the trunk, it was too heavy to handle alone.

"Ain't nobody but——"

Jodie reached down with a violent motion, clutched him over the face with the palm of his left hand, put his right knee in Goldy's back between the shoulder blades, jerked Goldy's head back against the pressure of his knee, and cut Goldy's taut black throat from ear to ear, straight down to the bone.

Goldy's scream mingled with the scream of the locomotive as the train thundered past overhead, shaking the entire tenement city. Shaking the sleeping black people in their lice-ridden beds. Shaking the ancient bones and the aching muscles and the t.b. lungs and the uneasy foetuses of unwed girls. Shaking plaster from the ceilings, mortar from between the bricks of the building walls. Shaking the rats between the walls, the cockroaches crawling over kitchen sinks and leftover food; shaking the sleeping flies hibernating in lumps like bees behind the casings of the windows. Shaking the fat, blood-filled bedbugs crawling over black skin. Shaking the fleas, making them hop. Shaking the sleeping dogs in their filthy pallets, the sleeping cats, the clogged toilets, loosening the filth.

Hank jumped aside just in time.

The blood spurted from Goldy's cut throat in a shower, spraying the black street, the front fender and front wheel of the hearse. It gleamed for an instant with a luminous red sheen on the black pavement. It dulled the next instant, turning dark, fading into deep purple. The first gushing stream slackened to a slow pumping fountain as the heart pumped out its last beats. The flesh of the wide bloody wound turned back like bleeding lips, frothing blood.

The sweet sickish perfume of fresh blood came up from the crap-smelling street, mingled with the foul tenement smell of Harlem.

Jodie stepped back and let the dying body flop on its back to the pavement, jerking and twisting inside the black gown in death convulsions as though having a frantic sex culmination with an unseen mate.

The thunder of the train diminished into the brackish sound of metal grinding on metal as the train braked for a stop at the 125th Street Station.

Jodie bent down and wiped his knife blade on the hem of

126

Goldy's black gown. The stroke had been executed so quickly there was blood only on the knife blade.

He straightened up, pressed the button releasing the catch. The blade dangled loose. With a twist of his wrist he snapped the knife shut. The lock clicked. He put it back into his coat-pocket.

"I bled that mother-raper like a boar hog," he said proudly.

"Talked himself into the grave."

As though by speechless accord, Hank and Jodie looked up and down the street, up at the window of the third-story flat, into the dimly lit hall, examined the windows of the surrounding tenements.

Nothing was moving.

CHAPTER 18

THE SHORT, sharp blast of a train whistle when it had crossed the river into Harlem awakened Jackson in a pool of terror.

He jumped to his feet, overturning the chair. He sensed someone striking at him from behind, ducked, and knocked the table aside. Wheeling about, he snatched the pipe from the table to knock Slim's brains out.

But there wasn't anybody.

"I must have been dreaming," he said to himself.

He realized then that he'd been asleep.

"There's a train coming," he said.

His wits were still fuddled.

He noticed his chauffeur's cap had fallen to the floor. He picked it up and brushed it off. But there was no dirt on it. The floor was spotlessly clean and still damp.

The scrubbed floor made him think of Imabelle. He wondered where she could have gone. To her sister's in the Bronx, maybe. But they were sure to find her there. The police were looking for her too. He'd have to phone her sister as soon as he got the gold ore checked in the baggage room at the station. He wasn't going to leave it at Goldy's, no matter what anyone said.

Suddenly he was filled with a sense of haste.

He searched his pockets for some paper to write Imabelle a note in case she came back there looking for him and didn't know where to find him. In his inside uniform pocket was a soiled sheet of stationery with Mr. Clay's letterhead containing a list of funeral items. He found a stub of pencil in his side overcoat pocket and unfolded the

128

paper onto the kitchen table. He scribbled hurriedly:

"Honey, look for my brother, Sister Gabriel, in front of Blumstein's. He'll tell you where I am at . . ."

He was about to sign his name when it occurred to him that Slim was coming back with Hank and Jodie.

"I ain't thinking at all," he muttered to himself, balled up the sheet of stationery and threw it into the corner.

The rising thunder of the approaching train brought back his nameless terror. He thought of a blues song his mother used to sing,

> I flag de train an' it keep on easing by
> I fold my arms; I hang my head an' cry.

Suddenly he was running without moving. He was running on the inside. He didn't have any time left to wonder where Imabelle had gone. Just time left to worry. Anyway, he'd gotten her away from Slim.

He picked up his club from the table. His eyes had turned red. His face was gray and dry, lips chapped.

An old gray rat poked his head from underneath the grease-covered rusty woodburning stove. The rat had red eyes also. The rat looked at Jackson and he looked at the rat.

The house began to shake. The floor was shaking, shaking the rat. Jackson felt himself begin to shake. His brains felt as though they were shaking up and down in his head, about to explode. The thunder of the train filled the room, froze the shaking man and shaking rat in a death-like trance.

At that moment the whistle screamed. It screamed like a stuck pig running through the corn patch with the knife still in it.

The rat vanished.

Jackson's feet began to run.

He ran blindly from the kitchen, through the bedroom, stumbling over the three-legged chair, jumped up and ran into the pitch-dark hall and started down the stairs.

Then he remembered Imabelle's clothes. He turned

129

around, ran back to the kitchen, laid his pipe on the table, gathered the clothes in his arms, turned around again and ran out of the flat, forgetting his club.

He ran through the dark hall, down the steep, dark stairs, trying to be as quiet as possible. Sweat started to pour from his dry skin. He could feel it trickling down his neck, from underneath his arms, down his sides, like crawling worms.

The hems of the dresses trailed on the dirty stairs. At the bottom of the first staircase he tripped over the skirts, fell belly-forward, holding the dresses clutched in his arms, and landed with a dull thud.

"Lord, my Savior," he muttered getting up. "Looks like I ain't got long to stay here."

He was hugging the dresses as though Imabelle were inside them, just able to see over the top of the pile, when he passed underneath the dim light in the ground-floor hall and came to the outside doorway.

He expected to see Goldy waiting impatiently on the front seat of the hearse. Instead he saw Hank and Jodie, standing on the far side of the hearse, facing each other and talking. He was petrified. He stood there with his mouth open in his wet black face, white teeth shining from purple-blue gums.

Hank and Jodie had just that instant withdrawn their gazes from the lighted hallway.

Hank was saying to Jodie, "Let's move him out the street."

"Move him where?"

"Inside the hearse."

"What for? Why don't we let the mother-raper lay where he's at?"

"He's a stooly. If the cops find him here they're on our trail like white on rice."

"If it was up to me, I'd leave him lay, and frig the cops. We're lamming, ain't we?"

Hank went back and opened the double-doors of the hearse. If he had turned his head he would have seen

Jackson standing petrified in the doorway. But he was looking at the body as he walked back.

"Grab his shoulders," he said, stooping to pick up the feet.

Jodie began putting on his gloves. He was looking at the body also.

"What the hell, you scared to touch him with your hands?"

"The mother-raper's dead. That's what I'm scared of."

Jackson thought they were preparing to move the trunk. The thought released his petrified muscles. Through the rim of his vision he saw the panel truck. He thought they were going to take the trunk and put it into the truck. He didn't have any way of stopping them. He didn't even have his club.

For the first time he realized that Goldy was nowhere in sight. Maybe Goldy had seen them coming and had hidden. Goldy had the revolver. Jackson felt like damning Goldy to everlasting hell, but didn't want to commit blasphemy on top of all the other sins he'd committed.

He backed quietly down the hall, half-stumbling at each step, turned at the foot of the stairs and started to run back upstairs to the flat. Then he thought better of it. After they'd moved the trunk into their truck, they might go up to the flat for something or other.

He looked about for a place to hide.

The space underneath the stairs had been walled in to form a closet with the door facing a small dark corner at the back of the hall. He backed into the corner, tried the door of the closet, found it opened.

Garbage cans were crammed helter-skelter among dirty mops and pails. Folding the dresses to keep them from dangling into the cans, he squeezed inside, silently closed the door, and stood in the stinking dark, scarcely breathing.

Jodie took the body beneath the armpits, Hank the feet. They rammed it feet first into the funeral paraphernalia underneath the trunk. It was a tight squeeze and they had to lay it on its back and push it, with their feet against the shoulders. Finally they got the head in far enough to close the doors.

Hank went back and picked up the white bonnet and gray wig and stuck it back on the head. Then he pulled down some of the black bunting and artificial wreaths to cover the head before shutting the door.

"What you doing that for?" Jodie asked.

"In case anybody looks."

"Who's going to look?"

"How the hell do I know? We can't lock it."

They turned and looked up at the window of the third-story flat again.

Jodie took off his gloves, stuck his bare hand into his pocket and gripped the handle of his knife.

"Who helped him, you reckon?"

"I don't figure it. I had it cased as her and Jackson, but this stooly makes it different."

"You reckon Jackson's in it too?"

"Got to be, I figure. It's his hearse."

"You reckon they're still upstairs?"

"We're going to see right soon."

They turned, crossed the sidewalk, and entered the hall. Both had their hands in their overcoat pockets, Hank's gripping his .38 automatic pistol, Jodie's gripping his bone-handled knife. Their eyes searched the shadows.

As they approached the stairs they were talking loudly enough for Jackson to hear from the stinking closet underneath.

"Double-crossing bitch, I should have killed her—"

"Shut up."

Jackson could hear each footstep touching lightly on the wooden floor. He held his breath.

"I don't care if she does hear me, she ain't got no place to hide."

"Shut up. Other people are in here who can hear."

Jackson heard the footsteps as they started to ascend the stairs. Suddenly one pair stopped.

"What you mean, shut up? I'm getting good-and-goddam tired of you telling me to shut up all the time."

The second pair of footsteps stopped just as abruptly.

"I mean shut up. Just that."

Jackson held his breath so long in the dangerous silence his lungs ached before the footsteps began ascending again.

No further words were spoken.

Jackson breathed softly, listening to the steps going higher and higher, becoming fainter. He gripped the doorknob, pulled it inward with all his strength, turned it slowly so as not to make a sound, and opened the door a crack with infinite caution.

He heard the footsteps start up the second staircase, barely hearing them when they moved along the third-story hall.

He waited a moment longer, then came out of the closet running. An empty garbage can turned over with a shattering clang. The sound kicked him down the hall with his arms full of dresses, like a pointed-toe shoe in his rump.

He heard feet pounding on the wooden floor of the upper hallway, hitting the wooden steps like a booted centipede. As he crossed the sidewalk he heard a window being opened overhead.

He grabbed at the handle of the hearse door, threw it open, tossed the dresses onto the seat, jumped inside, fumbled in his pocket for the ignition key, turned on the ignition, and pressed the starter button.

"Catch, you God-damned son of a bitch, Lord forgive me," he raved at the reluctant motor. "Catch, you mother-raping bastard son of a bitch of a God-damned car —Jesus Christ, I didn't mean it."

He saw Jodie coming down the dimly lit hall, growing bigger and bigger in the rectangular perspective.

"Lord, have mercy," Jackson prayed.

Jodie came out of the doorway in a long flying leap, the knife blade flashing in the gloom. He hit the pavement, skidded toward the curb, bent forward and flailing the air with both hands as if trying to halt his charge on the edge of a precipice, got his balance and turned as the old Cadillac motor roared.

Jackson shifted into drive and put weight on the treadle; the old hearse took off with a heavy whoomping sound, so fast the right edge of the front bumper hit the left rear-fender of the pickup truck before Jackson got control, bent the fender into a mangled fin that scratched a river of scars on the black side of the hearse as it roared past, barely missing an iron stanchion of the overhead trestle as it turned west into 130th Street.

"One more shave that close, Lord, and this brother ain't going to be here long," Jackson muttered as he wrapped his short fat arms about the wheel and watched the street come up over the hood.

CHAPTER 19

WHEN IMABELLE came downstairs and left Goldy and her man, Jackson, struggling with her trunk of gold ore, she glanced briefly at the parked hearse, giggled again, and started running down Park Avenue toward the 125th Street Station.

She didn't know the train schedule, but there would be a train leaving for Chicago.

"This sweet girl is going to be on it," she said to herself.

The 125th Street Station sat beneath the trestle like an artificial island, facing 125th Street. The double-track line widened into four tracks as it passed overhead on the gloomy, dimly-lit wooden platform. Passengers alighting there for the first time had the impulse to turn about and climb back into the train. The platform shook like palsy and the loose boards rattled like dry bones every time a train passed.

From the platform could be seen the lighted strip of 125th Street running across the island from the Triborough Bridge, connecting the Bronx and Brooklyn, to the 125th Street ferry across the Hudson River into New Jersey.

At street level the hot, brightly-lit waiting room was crammed with wooden benches, newsstands, lunch counters, slot machines, ticket windows, and aimless people. At the rear a double stairway ascended to the loading platform, with toilets underneath. Behind, out of sight, difficult to locate, impossible to get to, was the baggage room.

The surrounding area was choked with bars, flea-ridden flophouses called hotels, all-night cafeterias, hop dens,

135

whorehouses, gambling joints, catering to all the whims of nature.

Black and white folks rubbed shoulders day and night, over the beer-wet bars, getting red-eyed and rambunctious from the ruckus juice and fist-fighting in the street between the passing cars. They sat side by side in the neon glare of the food factories, eating things from the steam tables that had no resemblance to food.

Whores buzzed about the area like green flies over stewing chitterlings.

The whining voices of blues singers, coming from the nightmare-lighted jukeboxes, floated in noisome air:

> My mama told me when I was a chile
> Dat mens and whiskey would kill me after a while.

Muggers with scarred faces cased the lone pedestrians like hyenas watching lions feast.

Purse snatchers grabbed a poke and ran toward the dark beneath the trestle, trying to dodge the cops' bullets pinging against the iron stanchions. Sometimes they did, sometimes they didn't.

White gangsters, four and six together in the bullet-proof limousines, coming and going from the syndicate headquarters down the street, passed the harness cops in the patrol cars, giving them look for look.

Inside the station plainclothes detectives were on twenty-four hour duty. Outside on the street a patrol car was always in sight.

But Imabelle was more scared of Hank and Jodie than she was of the cops. She had never been mugged or fingerprinted. All the cops had ever wanted from her was a piece. Imabelle was a girl who believed that a fair exchange was no robbery.

She had her black coat buttoned tight, but running made the skirt flare, exposing a teasing strip of red dress.

A middle-aged church-going man, good husband and father of three school-age daughters, on his way to work, dressed in clean, starched overalls and an army jumper, heard the tapping of her heels on the pavement when he stepped from his ground-floor tenement.

"A mighty light-footed whore," he mumbled to himself.

When he came out onto the sidewalk he looked around and saw the flash of her high-yellow face and the tantalizing strip of red skirt in the spill of street light. He caught a sudden live-wire edge. He couldn't help it. His wife had been ailing and he hadn't had his ashes hauled in God knows when. As he looked at that fine yaller gal tripping his way, his teeth shone in his black face like a lighthouse on the sea.

"You is for me, baby," he said in a big bass voice, grabbing her by the arm. He was willing to put out five bucks.

Without breaking the flow of her motion she smacked him in his face with her black pocketbook.

The blow startled him more than it hurt. He hadn't meant her any harm; he just wanted to give the girl a play. But when he thought about a whore hitting a church man like himself, he became enraged. He closed in and clutched her.

"Don't you hit me, whore."

"Turn me loose, you black mother-raper," she fumed, struggling furiously in his grip.

He was a garbage collector and strong as a horse. She couldn't break free.

"Don't cuss me, whore, 'cause I'm going to get some of you whether you like it or not," he mouthed in a red raving passion of rage and lust, aiming to throw her to the pavement and rape her then and there.

"You going to get some of your mama, you big mother-raper," she cursed, digging a switchblade knife, similar to Jodie's, from her coat pocket. She slashed him across the cheek.

He jumped back, clinging to her with one hand, and felt his cheek with the other. He took away his bloody hand and looked at the blood on it. He looked surprised. It was his own blood.

"You cut me, you whore," he said in a surprised voice.

137

"I'll cut you again, you mother-raper," she said, and began slashing at him in a feminine fury.

He released her and backed away, striking at the knife with his bare hands as though trying to beat off a wasp.

"What's the matter with you, whore?" he was saying, but his voice was drowned by the thunder of a train approaching the station. Suddenly the whistle blew like a human scream.

It scared her so much she jumped back and stared at the slashed man as though it had been he who had screamed.

"I'll kill you, you whore," he said, preparing to charge her knife.

She knew she couldn't make him run, couldn't cut him down, and if he overpowered her he'd kill her. She turned and ran toward the station, swinging the open knife.

He ran after her, trailing blood from his face and hands.

"Don't let 'im catch you, baby," someone called encouragement from the dark.

The train overtook them, thundered by overhead, shaking the earth, shaking her running ass, shaking the blood from his wounds like scattered rain drops. It started grinding to a stop. The thunder terrified her; the brackish sound filled her mouth with acid.

She threw the knife into the gutter and ran past the line of waiting taxicabs, the cruising whores, the colored loiterers; turned, without stopping, through the side entrance into the waiting room, ran back to the women's toilet underneath the stairs, and locked herself inside.

The motley group of people standing about, sitting on the wooden benches, scarcely paid any attention. It wasn't unusual to see a woman running in that area.

But when the man hit the door, bleeding like a stuck bull, everybody sat up.

"I'm going to kill dat whore," he raved as he burst into the waiting room.

A colored brother looked at him and said, "She sho gave him some love-licks."

138

The man was halfway to the toilet when the white detective ran up and clutched him by both arms.

"Hold on, Brother Jones, hold on. What's the trouble?"

The man twisted in the detective's grip, but didn't break free.

"Listen, white folks, I don't want no trouble. That whore cut me and I'm going to get some of her."

"Hold on, hold on, brother. If she cut you we'll get her. But you're not going to get anybody. Understand?"

The colored detective sauntered up, looked indifferently at the bleeding man.

"Who cut him?"

"He said some woman did."

"Where'd she go?"

"She ran into the women's toilet."

The colored detective asked the cut man, "What does she look like?"

"Bright woman in a black coat and a red dress."

The colored detective laughed.

"Better let those bright whores alone, Daddy-o."

He turned, laughing, and went back toward the women's toilet.

Two uniformed cops from a patrol car came in quickly, as if expecting trouble. They looked disappointed when they didn't find any.

"Call the ambulance, will you?" the white detective said to one of them.

The cop hastened out to the patrol car to call the police ambulance on the two-way radio. The other cop just stood.

People gathered in a circle to stare at the big cut black man dripping red blood on the brown tiled floor. A porter came up with a wet mop and looked disapprovingly at the bloody floor.

Nobody thought it was unusual. It happened once or twice every night in that station. The only thing missing was that no one was dead.

"What did she cut you for?" the white detective asked.

"Just mean, that's why. She's just a mean whore."

The detective looked as though he agreed.

The colored detective found the toilet door locked. He knocked. "Open up, Bright-eyes."

No one answered. He knocked again.

"It's the law, honey. Don't make me have to get the stationmaster to get this door open or papa's going to be rough."

The inside bolt was slipped back. He pushed and the door opened.

Imabelle faced him from the mirror. She had washed and powdered her face, straightened her hair, rouged her lips, wiped off her high-heeled black suede shoes, and looked as though she'd just stepped from a band box.

He flashed his badge and grinned at her.

She said complainingly, "Can't a lady clean up a little in this joint without you cops busting in?"

He looked around. The only other occupants were two white women of middle age, who were cowering in a far corner.

"Are you the woman who's having trouble with that man?" he asked Imabelle, trying to trick a confession from her.

She didn't go for it. "Having trouble with what man?" She screwed up her face and looked indignant. "I came in here to clean up. I don't know what you're talking about."

"Come on, Baby, don't give papa any trouble," he said, looking her over as though he might consider laying her.

She gave him a look from her big brown bedroom eyes and flashed her pearly smile as though it might be a good consideration.

"If any man says he's having trouble with me, you can just say that's his own fault."

"I know just what you mean, Baby, but you shouldn't have cut him."

"I ain't cut nobody," she said, switching out into the waiting room.

"That's the whore who cut me," the man said, pointing a finger dripping with blood.

The morbid crowd turned to stare at her.

"Man, I'd have cut her first," some joker said. "If you know what I mean."

Imabelle ignored the crowd as she pushed her way forward. She walked up and faced the cut man and looked him straight in the face.

"This the man you mean?" she asked the colored detective.

"That's the one who's cut."

"I ain't never seen this man before in my life."

"You lying whore!" the man shouted.

"Take it easy, Daddy-o," the colored detective warned.

"What'd I cut you for, if I cut you?" Imabelle challenged.

The onlookers laughed.

One colored brother quoted:

Black gal make a freight train jump de track.
But a yaller gal make a preacher Ball de Jack.

"Come on, where's the knife?" the white detective said to Imabelle. "I'm getting tired of this horseplay."

"I'd better search the washroom," the colored detective said.

"She throwed it away outside," the cut man said, "I seen her throw it into the street, before she ran inside."

"Why didn't you pick it up?" the detective asked.

"Who for?" the cut man asked in surprise. "I don't need no knife to kill that whore. I can kill her with my hands."

The detective stared at him.

"For evidence. You say she cut you."

"Let's get it," one of the patrol cops said to the other and they went outside to look for the knife.

"Course she cut me. You can see for yourself," the cut man said.

The crowd laughed and started drifting away.

"Do you want to make a charge against this woman?"

"Charge? I'm charging her now. You can see for yourself she cut me."

141

Some joker said, "If she didn't cut you, you better see a doctor about those leaky veins."

"What are you holding me for?" Imabelle said to the white detective. "I tell you I ain't never seen this man before. He's got me mistaken for somebody else."

Another team of patrol-car cops came on the scene, looking at the cut black man with the curiosity of whites as they drew off their heavy gloves.

"You are to take these people to the precinct," the white detective said. "The man wants to enter a charge of assault against this woman."

"Jesus, I don't want him bleeding all over the car," one of the cops complained.

The whine of an ambulance sounded from the distance.

"Here comes the ambulance now," the colored detective said.

"Why they going to take me in when I haven't done anything?" Imabelle appealed to him.

He looked at her sympathetically. "I feel for you but I can't reach you, Baby," he said.

"If you prove your innocence you can sue him for false arrest," the white detective said.

"Well, ain't that something?" she said angrily.

Outside, the two uniformed cops searched in the gutter for the missing knife. Two colored men standing on the sidewalk watched them silently.

Finally one of the cops thought to ask them, "Did either of you men see anyone pick up a knife around here?"

"I seen a colored boy pick it up," one of the men admitted.

The cops reddened.

"God damn it, didn't you see us looking for it?" one asked angrily.

"You didn't say what you was looking for, Boss."

"By this time the bastard is probably blocks away," the second cop complained.

"Where'd he go?" the first cop asked.

The man pointed up Park Avenue.

Both cops gave him a hard threatening look.

"What did he look like?"

The colored man turned to his companion.

"What he look like, you think?"

The second colored man disapproved of his companion's volunteering information to white cops about a colored boy.

"I didn't seen him," he said, showing his disapproval.

Both cops turned to stare at him in rage.

"You didn't seen him," one mimicked. "Well, God damn it, you're both under arrest."

The cops escorted the two colored men around to the front of the station and put them on the back seat of their patrol car while they got into the front seat. Passersby glanced at them with brief curiosity, and passed on.

The cops turned the car up Park Avenue on the wrong side to show their power. The red light beamed like an evil eye. They drove slowly, flashing the adjustable spotlights along the sidewalks, into the faces of pedestrians, into doorways, cracks, corners, vacant lots, searching for a colored boy who had picked up a bloodstained knife among the half-million colored people in Harlem.

They were just in time to see a panel delivery truck with a mangled rear fender turn the corner into 130th Street, but they weren't interested in it.

"What shall we do with these black sons of bitches?" one of the cops asked the other.

"Let 'em go."

The driver stopped the car and said, "Get out."

The two colored men got out and walked back toward the station.

When they arrived the ambulance was driving off, taking the cut man to Harlem Hospital so his wounds could be stitched before sending him on to the precinct station to prefer charges against Imabelle.

At the same time the patrol car carrying Imabelle to the precinct station was going east on 125th Street. It passed a hearse that turned slowly from Madison Avenue. But there was nothing suspicious about a hearse traveling about the streets in the early hours of morning. Folks were dying in Harlem at all hours.

The patrol cops turned Imabelle over to the desk sergeant to be held until the cut man came to prefer charges.

"You mean I've got to stay here until—"

"Shut up and sit down." The desk sergeant cut her off in a bored voice.

She started to act indignant, thought better of it, crossed the room to one of the wooden benches against the wall, and sat quietly with crossed legs showing six inches of creamy yellow thighs, as she contemplated her red-lacquered fingernails.

While she was sitting there, Grave Digger came out of the captain's office. He wore a white patch of bandage beneath his pushed-back hat and an expression of unadulterated danger. He looked at Imabelle casually, then did a double-take, recognizing her. He walked slowly across the room and looked down at her.

She gave him her bedroom look, hitched her red skirt higher, exposing more of her creamy yellow thighs.

"Well, bless my big flat feet," he said. "Baby-o, I got news for you."

She gave him her pearly smile of promise of pleasant things to come.

He slapped her with such savage violence it spun her out of the chair to land in a grotesque splay-legged posture on her belly on the floor, the red dress hiked so high it showed the black nylon panties she wore.

"And that ain't all," he said.

144

CHAPTER 20

WHEN JACKSON turned into 125th Street from Madison Avenue, headed toward the station baggage-room, he was driving as cautiously as if the street were paved with eggs.

He was in a slow sweat from the crown of his burr head to the white soles of his black feet. Worrying about Imabelle, wondering if that woman of his was safe, worrying about her trunk full of gold ore, hoping nothing would go wrong now that he had rescued it from those thugs.

He was steering with one hand, crossing himself with the other.

One moment he was praying, "Lord, don't quit me now."

The next he was moaning the lowdown blues:

> If trouble was money
> I'd be a millionaire. . . .

A patrol car passed him, headed toward the precinct station, going like a bat out of hell. It went by so fast he didn't see Imabelle in the back seat. He thought they were taking some thug to jail. He hoped it was that bastard Slim.

An ambulance shot past. He skinned his eyes, his sweat turning cold, trying to see who was riding in it, and almost rammed into a taxi ahead. He caught a glimpse of the silhouette of a man and was relieved. Weren't Imabelle, whoever it was.

He wondered where that woman of his could be. He was worrying so hard about her that he almost ran down a big

145

fat black man doing the locomotive shuffle diagonally across the street.

> Stood on the corner with her feets soaking wet
> Begging each and every man she met . . .

Jackson eased the hearse past Big Fats as though he were picking his way through a brier patch. He didn't open his mouth again. Couldn't tell what a drunk might do next. He didn't want any trouble until he got the trunk checked and safe from Goldy.

He had to drive past the front of the station, circle it on Park Avenue, and come down beside the baggage room entrance from the rear.

By the time he had pulled to the curb before the baggage-room door, behind the line of loading taxicabs, Big Fats had navigated the dangerous rapids of 125th Street traffic and was shuffling up the crowded sidewalk beside the lighted windows of the waiting room, heading up Park Avenue toward the Harlem River.

None of them said anything to Big Fats. No need to borrow trouble with an able-bodied colored drunk the size of Big Fats. Especially if his eyes were red. That's the way race riots were started.

But it made Jackson nervous to have the police congregating in the vicinity while he was checking the trunk of gold ore. He was so nervous as it was he was jumping from his shadow. He left the motor running from habit. When he got out to go to the baggage room, Big Fats spied him.

"Little brother!" Big Fats shouted, shuffling up to Jackson and putting his big fat arm about Jackson's short fat shoulders.

"Short-black-and-fat like me. You tell 'em, short and fatty. Can't trust no fat man, can they?"

Jackson threw the arm off angrily and said, "Why don't you behave yourself. You're a disgrace to the race."

Big Fats put the locomotive in reverse, let it idle on the track, building up steam.

146

"What race, Little Brother. You want to race?"

"I mean our race. You know what I mean."

Big Fats bucked his red-veined eyes at Jackson in amazement.

"You mean to say you'd let 'em trust you with they women?" he shouted.

"Go get sober," Jackson shouted back with uncontrollable irritation, went around Big Fats like skirting a mountain, hurried into the baggage room without looking back.

Big Fats forgot him instantly, began shuffling up the street again.

Jackson found a colored porter.

"I got a trunk I want to check."

The porter looked at Jackson and became angry just because Jackson had spoken to him.

"Where you going to?" he asked gruffly.

"Chicago."

"Where's your ticket at?"

"I ain't got my ticket yet. I just want to check my trunk until I get my ticket."

The porter went into a raving fury.

"Can't check no trunk nowhere if you ain't got no ticket," he shouted at the top of his voice. "Don't you know that?"

"What are you getting so mad about? You act like we're God's angry people."

The porter hunched his shoulders as though he were going to take a punch at Jackson.

"I ain't mad. Does I look mad?"

Jackson backed away.

"Listen, I don't want to check it nowhere. I just want to check it here until I come down tonight to get my ticket."

"You don't want to check it nowhere. Man, what's the matter with you?"

"If you don't want to check it I'll go see the man," Jackson threatened.

The man was the white baggage-master.

The porter didn't want any trouble with the man.

"You means you want to check it," he said, giving in

grudgingly. "Why didn't you say you just wanted to check it instead of coming in here talking 'bout going to Chicago?"

He snatched up a hand truck as though he'd take it and beat Jackson's brains out with it.

"Where's it at?"

"Outside."

The porter wheeled the hand truck onto the sidewalk and looked up and down the street.

"I don't see no trunk."

"It's in the hearse there."

He looked through the windows of the hearse and saw the trunk on the coffin rack.

"What you doing carrying a trunk around in a hearse for?" he asked suspiciously.

"We use it to carry everything."

"Well, get it out then," the porter said, still suspicious. "I ain't checking no trunk in no hearse where dead folks has been."

"Aw, man, Lord in heaven. Don't be so evil. The trunk's heavy. Ain't you going to help me lift it down?"

"I don't get paid for unloading no trunks from no hearses. I checks 'em when they is on the street."

"I'll help you git it out," a colored loiterer offered.

Jackson and the loiterer walked to the back of the hearse. The porter followed. Two white taxi drivers, taking a break, looked on curiously. From down the sidewalk a white cop eyed the group absently.

Big Fats came shuffling back down the street just as Jackson swung open the double doors of the hearse.

"Watch out!" he shouted. "Can't trust no fat man!"

Jackson, the porter, and the third colored man stepped back from the hearse in unison as though they had suddenly looked upon the naked face of the devil.

Big Fats shuffled closer, looked over Jackson's shoulder. The locomotive stopped dead on the tracks.

All four black men had turned putty-gray.

"Great Gawdamighty!" Big Fats shouted. "Look at that!"

Underneath the trunk black cloth was piled high. Artificial flowers were scattered about in garish disarray. A horseshoe wreath of artificial lilies had slipped to the back. Looking out from the arch of white lilies was a black face. The face was looking backward from a head-down position, resting on the back of the skull. A white bonnet sat atop a gray wig which had fallen askew. The face wore a horrible grimace of pure evil. White-walled eyes stared at the four gray men with a fixed, unblinking stare. Beneath the face was the huge purple-lipped wound of a cut throat.

Jackson felt his scalp ripple as he recognized the face of his brother Goldy. His mouth came half open and caught. His eyes stretched until he felt as though the eyeballs were hanging from the sockets. His jaws began to ache. A warm wet stream flowed suddenly down his pants leg.

"That's a dead body, ain't it?" the porter said in a cracked voice, as though his suspicions had suddenly come true. His own eyes were as white-walled and fixed as the eyes of the corpse.

"Where?" Jackson said.

His brain had gone numb with panic and fear. His whole fat body began to shake as though he had the ague.

"Where?" the porter shrilled in a high whining voice that sounded like a file scraping across a saw. "Right there, that's where!"

The third colored man was still backing up the street.

"Cut sidewise to the bone," Big Fats said in a hushed, awed voice.

The taxi drivers sauntered over and looked down at the gory black head.

"Jesus Christ!" one exclaimed.

"It's a wig," the other one said.

"What is?"

"See, there's short hair underneath. By God, it's a man."

The uniformed cop approached slowly like a forerunner of doom, nonchalantly twirling his white nightstick. He looked down into the hearse with the air of a man who has been washed with all waters. The next instant he drew back in pallid shock and sucked in his breath. This was the water he'd never seen.

"How did this get there? Who did this? Whose hearse is this?" he asked stupidly, trying to collect his wits and looking quickly about for help.

He caught the eye of one of the plainclothes detectives at the waiting-room entrance and beckoned to him.

The third colored man had kept backing up Park Avenue toward the dark until he considered it safe to turn around. Now he was running up the dark street as fast as his feet would carry him.

Big Fats had turned cold sober and was trying to inch away too when the cop said sharply, "Don't anybody leave here."

"I ain't leaving," Big Fats denied. "Just stretching my feet a little."

The white taxicab drivers backed away and stood shoulder to shoulder against the baggage-room wall.

The white plainclothes detective pushed the porter aside, saying, "What's this?"

He took a look into the hearse, turned pale. "What the hell is this?"

"A body," the cop said.

"Who's the driver?"

"Me, boss," Jackson quavered.

The harness cop blew out his breath in a sighing sound, glad to let the plainclothes detective take over. A crowd had begun to gather and he was glad to find something he could do.

"Get back!" he ordered. "Stand back!"

The detective took out his notebook and pencil.

"What's your name?" he asked Jackson.

"Jackson."

"Who's your boss?"

"Mr. H. Exodus Clay, on 134th Street."

"Where'd you pick up this corpse?"

"I don't know, boss. It was in there when I got in. I swear 'fore God."

150

The detective suddenly stopped writing and stared at Jackson incredulously.

Everyone stared at him.

"He say he done found a stiff and don't know where it come from," someone in the crowd exclaimed.

Jackson was trembling so that his teeth were chattering like ratchets. He wasn't scared now of losing his woman or losing her gold ore. He wasn't thinking about his woman or her gold. He was thinking only of his brother lying there in death with his throat cut. This was the instinctive fear of the violently dead. Fear of the dead themselves. He hadn't started yet thinking about what was going to happen to him. But the detective's next question made him think about it.

"Do you mean to say you didn't know this corpse was in the hearse when you took it out?"

"No sir. I swear 'fore God."

The colored detective came up at that moment and said casually, "What's the beef about?"

A patrol car turned in from 125th Street, driving on the wrong side, plowed a path through the crowd that was spreading across the street.

"He's got a corpse in there and he says he doesn't know how it got there," the white detective replied.

"Couldn't have walked, that's for sure," the colored detective said, pushing between Jackson and the porter to look at the corpse.

"I'll be a mother-for-you!" he exclaimed, half choking, more repulsed by sight of the cut throat than shocked.

Then he looked more closely.

"That's Sister Gabriel. And that son of a bitch was a man all this time!"

The white detective continued to question Jackson as though he were uninterested in the corpse's sex.

"How did it happen that you took the hearse out without knowing there was a corpse in it?"

"Boss told me to bring this trunk to the station and check it." He talked in gasps, scarcely able to breathe.

"Swear 'fore God. I just brought the trunk down like he told me to do and put it there on the rack and drove on here to the station, like he told me to. Lord be my judge."

"Check the trunk for what?"

Behind them the patrol-car cops were pushing back the crowd.

"Get back, get back!"

The gray had left Jackson's face and he had begun to sweat again. He wiped the sweat from his face, dabbing at his red-veined eyes with the dirty handkerchief.

"I didn't understand you, boss."

Bums and prostitutes and working johns and loiterers and the night thieves and bindle stiffs and blind beggars and all the flotsam that floated on the edges of the station like dirty scum on bog water were jostling each other, drawn by the word of a cut-throat corpse, trying to get a look to see what they were missing.

"I said what does he want to check the trunk for?"

"For Chicago. He's going to Chicago tonight and he wanted to check his trunk now so when he got his ticket he wouldn't be bothered with it," Jackson said gaspingly.

The white detective snapped shut his notebook.

"I don't believe a God-damned word of that bullshit."

"It could be true," the colored detective said. "One driver might have brought in the corpse and left it in the hearse for a moment and this driver—"

"But God damnit, who's checking a trunk at this time of night?"

The colored detective laughed. "This is Harlem. His boss might have the trunk stuffed with hundred-dollar bills."

"Well, I'll soon find out. You hold him. If he got the corpse legitimately, it was released by the homicide bureau." He looked about, over the heads of the crowd. "Where the hell's that patrol car? I'm going to contact the precinct station."

Suddenly Jackson could see the electric chair and himself sitting in it. If they took him to the precinct station they'd find out about Slim and his gang. And they'd find out about Coffin Ed getting blinded and Grave Digger getting

152

hurt, maybe killed. They'd find out about the gold ore and about Goldy and about him stealing the five hundred dollars and stealing the hearse too. They'd find out that Goldy was his brother and they'd figure that Goldy was trying to steal his woman's gold ore. And they'd figure he'd cut Goldy's throat. And they'd burn his black ass to a cinder.

"I've seen the order," he said, inching toward the sidewalk. "It was on the front seat, but I didn't know who it was for."

"Order?" the white detective snapped. "Order for what?"

"Order for the body. We get an order from the police to take the body. I saw it right there on the front seat."

"Well, God damnit, why didn't you say so? Let's see it."

Jackson went to the front of the hearse and opened the door. He looked on the bare seat.

"It was right here," he said.

He crawled halfway into the driver's compartment on his hands and knees, groping behind the seat, looking on the floor. He heard the old Cadillac motor turning over softly. He inched half of his rump onto the seat to lean over and look into the glove compartment. His elbow touched the gear lever and knocked it over to drive, but the motor purred softly and the car didn't move.

"It was right here just a minute ago," he repeated.

Now both detectives stood on the sidewalk by the door, eying him skeptically.

"Contact precinct and inquire about a recent homicide," the white detective called to a patrol-car cop. "Colored man impersonating a nun got his throat slashed. See if the body was released. Get the name of the undertaker."

"Right-o," the cop said, hurrying off to his two-way radio.

Jackson got all of his rump onto the seat in order to search on top of the sunshades where a stack of papers were shelved.

"It was right here. I saw it."

He put his right hand on the wheel to steady himself to get a better look. Suddenly, with his left hand he slammed the door shut; he put his whole weight down on the gas treadle.

The old Cadillac motor was the last of the '47 models with the big cylinder-bore and had enough power to pull a loaded freight train.

The deep-throated roar of the big-bored cylinders sounded like a four-motor stratocruiser gaining altitude as the big black hearse took off.

Pedestrians were scattered in grotesque flight. A blind man jumped over a bicycle trying to get out of the way.

There was a nine-foot gap between a big trailer-truck going east toward the bridge and a taxi going west on 125th Street. Jackson put the hearse in a straight line across the street and it went through that nine-foot hole so fast it didn't touch, straight down the narrow lane of Park Avenue beside the iron stanchions of the overhead trestle. The gearshift was clumping as it climbed into second, third, and hit the supercharger.

Pistols went off around the station like firecrackers on a Chinese New Year's day.

The soft mewling yowl of the patrol car sounded and swelled swiftly into a raving scream as the first of the patrol cars leaped into pursuit. It headed straight toward the side of the big trailer-truck as the cop tried to calculate the speed; he calculated wrong and skidded as he tried to turn. The patrol car went into the big, high, corrugated-steel trailer broadside, tried to go underneath it, was flipped back into the street, and spun to a stop with the front wheels bent out of use.

The two other patrol cars were just beginning to whine. Over and above the din of noise was the big jubilant crowing of Big Fats.

"What did I tell you? Can't trust no fat man! That little fat mother-raper done cut his own mama's throat from ear to ear!"

CHAPTER 21

GRAVE DIGGER stood over the prone figure of Imabelle in a blind rage. That acid-throwing bastard's woman, trying to play cute with him. And his partner, Coffin Ed, was in the hospital, maybe blinded for life. The air was electric with his rage.

He was wearing Coffin Ed's pistol along with his own. He had it in his hand without knowing he had drawn it. He had his finger on the hair-trigger, and it was all he could do to keep from blowing off some chunks of her fancy yellow prat.

Two harness cops, passing through the booking room, turned tentatively in his direction to restrain him, saw the pistol trembling in his hand, then drew up in silent amazement.

Two patrol cops bringing in three drunken prostitutes stopped, staring wide-eyed. The loud cursing voices of the prostitutes were cut off in mid-sentence. They seemed to shrink bodily, stood suspended in cowed postures, became sober on the spot.

Everyone in the room thought Grave Digger was going to kill Imabelle.

The silence lasted until Imabelle scrambled hastily to her feet and glared at Grave Digger with a rage equal to his own.

"What the hell's the matter with you, cop?" she shouted.

She was in such a fury she forgot to pull down her skirt and brush the dust from her clothes.

"If you open your mouth once more—" Grave Digger began.

"Easy does it," the desk sergeant said, cutting him off.

Imabelle's left cheek was bright red and swelling. Her hair was disarranged. Her eyes were cat-yellow, her mouth a mangled scar in a face gone bulldog ugly.

The harness cops looked at her sympathetically.

Grave Digger controlled himself with an effort. His motions were jerky as he holstered the pistol. His tall, lank frame moved erratically, like a puppet on strings. He couldn't trust himself to look at her again. He turned toward the desk sergeant.

"What's the rap on this woman?" His voice was thick.

"Cutting up a man over at the 125th Street station."

"Bad?"

"Naw. A colored worker who lives back of the station in the bucket says she slashed him."

Grave Digger finally turned back and looked at Imabelle as if to question her, then changed his mind.

"They took him to Harlem Hospital to get stitched," the desk sergeant added. "They'll bring him in shortly to prefer charges."

"I want her," Grave Digger said in a flat voice.

The desk sergeant looked at Grave Digger's face.

"Take her," he said.

At the same time he buzzed the captain's office from the row of button signals on his desk. He didn't want to argue with Grave Digger, but he couldn't let him take the prisoner out of the station without orders.

The lieutenant who was on night duty came from the captain's office and asked, "Yeah?"

The desk sergeant nodded toward Grave Digger and Imabelle.

"Jones wants this pickup."

"She was at the whing-ding up on the river tonight," Grave Digger said thickly.

"What do you want her for?"

"She going to show me where to find them."

The lieutenant looked as though he didn't like the idea too well.

"What's on her in the book?" he asked the desk sergeant.

"A colored man says she cut him. Over on Park Avenue, in the bucket. Haven't brought him in yet."

The lieutenant turned back to Grave Digger.

"Any connection?"

"She's going to tell me," Grave Digger said in his thick, cottony voice.

"I ain't cut nobody," Imabelle said, "I ain't never seen that man before in my life."

"Shut up," the desk sergeant said.

The lieutenant looked her over carefully.

"Strictly penitentiary bait," he muttered angrily, thinking. It's these high-yellow bitches like her that cause these black boys to commit so many crimes.

"It's getting late," Grave Digger said.

The lieutenant frowned. It was irregular, and he didn't like any irregularities on his shift. But hoodlums had thrown acid in a cop's eyes. This was one of the hoodlums' women. And this was the cop's partner.

"Take her," he said. "Take somebody with you. Take O'Malley."

"I don't want anybody with me," Grave Digger said. "I got Ed's pistol with me, and that's enough."

The lieutenant turned without saying another word and went back into the captain's office.

None of the other cops said anything. They stared from Grave Digger to Imabelle.

Grave Digger walked up to her. She stood her ground defiantly. He snapped handcuffs on her wrists so quickly she didn't know what was happening. When he took her by the arm and began steering her toward the door, she turned and appealed to the desk sergeant.

"Are you going to let this crazy man take me away from here?"

The desk sergeant looked away without replying.

"I got my rights——" she shouted.

Grave Digger jerked her through the door so violently

that her feet flew out from under her. He dragged her down the concrete steps.

His car was parked half a block down the street.

"Turn me loose. I can walk," she said, and he freed her arm.

The car was the same black sedan in which he had followed Gus's Cadillac to the gang's hideaway on the river. He opened the front door. She got in awkwardly, hindered by the handcuffs. He went around and got into the driver's seat.

"All right, where are they?"

"I don't know where they're at," she said sulkily.

He turned on the seat to face her.

"Don't play cute with me, woman. I want those acid-throwing bastards and you're going to take me to them or I'll pistol-whip your face until no man ever looks at you again." His voice was so thick she could barely understand him.

She felt the danger emanating from him. She might have still defied him if he had threatened to kill her. She wanted to get away herself before Hank and Jodie were caught and made to talk. Nothing could be done to her without their testimony. But she knew he meant what he said about destroying her face.

"I'll take you where they live. I want 'em caught. But I don't know whether they're still there. They might have lammed already."

He started the motor, tuned in the short-wave radio to the police signal.

"Where is it?"

"In a rooming house up on St. Nicholas Avenue, over a doctor's. He lives in the first two floors and rents out the top two to roomers."

"I know where it is and you'd better pray that they're still there."

She had nothing to say to that.

As they turned north on St. Nicholas Avenue, a metallic voice from the radio said,

". . . pick up a black open-face hearse; 1947 Cadillac;

158

M-series license, number unknown, driven by short, black-skinned Negro wearing chauffeur's uniform. . . . Dark green steamer trunk riding on coffin carrier visible through side windows, containing corpse of male Negro dressed in nun's habit. Known as Sister Gabriel. Slashed throat. . . . Hearse heading south on Park Avenue. . . . Over. . . . Repeat. . . . Pick up—"

"That complicates matters." Grave Digger knew immediately that Jackson was driving the hearse. It had to be one of Clay's hearses. Somehow the gang had gotten to Goldy. But why was Jackson running from the police?

Imabelle shuddered, thinking of how close she'd come to getting her own throat cut.

Grave Digger took a shot in the dark. "Where did you contact Jackson?"

"I haven't seen Jackson."

"What's in the trunk?"

"Gold ore."

He didn't look around.

They were going fast up the wet black pavement of St. Nicholas Avenue. On the east side of the street were rows of apartment buildings, becoming larger, more spacious, better kept; facing the steep cliff of the rocky park across the street. Above was the university plateau, overlooking the Hudson River.

"I haven't got time to put it together now. I'm going to get the bastards first and put it together afterward."

"I hope you kill 'em," she said viciously.

"You're going to have a lot to talk to me about later, Little Sister."

Day was breaking. The buildings high up on the plateau stood out in the morning light.

They passed the intersection of 145th Street with the subway kiosks on each corner. The car made a sickening dip and rose sharply into the section where the elite of the underworld lived among the working strivers.

A delivery truck was dumping stacks of the *Daily News* onto the wet sidewalk. Next to the drugstore was an all-night barbecue-joint, the counter stools filled with early

159

workers in the glaring neon light, eating barbecued ribs for breakfast. The hot pork-ribs turned on four automatic spits before a huge electric grill built into the wall near the plate-glass front window, tended by a tall black man in a white chef's uniform.

Two doors beyond Eddie's Cellar Restaurant she pointed toward a yellow hardtop Roadmaster Buick, parked beneath a street light in front of a four-storied stone-fronted house.

"There's their car."

Grave Digger pulled in ahead, skidded to a stop, got out and looked at the dark front windows of the house. At street level was a black lacquered door with a shiny brass knocker. Three white enamel door bells were placed in a vertical row on the red door frame beneath a black-and-white plaque bearing the name of Dr. J. P. Robinson.

The house was asleep.

Grave Digger walked quickly back to the car, casing the street as he went and memorizing the number on the yellow California license plate. First he opened the engine hood, disconnected the wires from the distributor head and put it into his coat pocket, and slammed the hood down with a bang. Then he tried the doors, found them locked, and peered inside. There was a tan cowhide suitcase in back on the floor. He went around to the luggage compartment, sprung the lock with the screwdriver blade from his heavy jackknife, glanced briefly at the luggage stacked inside, pushed the lid down and walked back to his car. The operation hadn't taken more than a minute.

"Where are they?"

"At Billie's."

"All three of them?"

She nodded. "If they haven't left."

He got into his seat behind the wheel, looked up the black macadam surface of St. Nicholas rising in a wide black stripe between rows of fashionable apartment buildings on both sides, taking gray shape in the morning light.

Early workers were trudging in from the side streets, hurrying toward the subway. Later the downtown office-porters would pour from the crowded flats in a steady stream, carrying polished leather briefcases stuffed with overalls to look like businessmen, and buy the *Daily News* to read on the subway.

The men he was looking for were not in sight.

"Who has the habit?" he asked.

"Both of 'em. Hank and Jodie, I mean. Hank's on hop and Jodie on heroin."

"How about the slim one?"

"He just drinks."

"What monickers are they using with Billie?"

"Hank calls himself Morgan; Jodie—Walker; Slim—Goldsmith."

"Then Billie knows about their gold-mine pitch?"

"I don't think so."

"Woman, there are a thousand questions you're going to have to answer," he said as he shifted into gear and got the car to moving again.

They went past Lucky's Cabaret, King-of-the-Chicken restaurant, Elite Barbershop, the big stone private mansion known as Harlem's Castle, made a U-turn at 155th Street between the subway kiosks, came back past The Fat Man's Bar and Grill, and drew up before the entrance to a large swank six-storied gray-stone apartment-building. Big expensive cars lined the curbs in that area.

From there, going down the steep descent of 155th Street to the bridge, it was less than a five-minute walk to that dark, dismal section along the Harlem River where the shooting fracas had taken place.

CHAPTER 22

WHEN JACKSON took off in the big old Cadillac hearse down Park Avenue, he didn't know where he was going. He was just running. He clung to the wheel with both hands. His bulging eyes were set in a fixed stare on the narrow strip of wet brick pavement as it curled over the hood like an apple-peeling from a knife blade, as though he were driving underneath it. On one side the iron stanchions of the trestle flew past like close-set fence pickets, on the other the store-fronted sidewalk made one long rushing somber kaleidoscope in the gray light before dawn.

The deep, steady thunder of the supercharger spilled out behind. The open back-doors swung crazily on the bumpy road, battering the head of the corpse as it jolted up and down beneath the bouncing trunk.

He headed into the red traffic-light at 116th Street doing eighty-five miles an hour. He didn't see it. A sleepy taxi driver saw something black go past in front of him and thought he was seeing automobile ghosts.

The stalls of the Harlem Market underneath the railroad trestle begin at 115th Street and extend down to 101st Street. Delivery trucks filled with meat, vegetables, fruit, fish, canned goods, dried beans, cotton goods, clothing, were jockeying back and forth in the narrow lane between the stanchions and the sidewalk. Laborers, stall-keepers, truck jumpers and drivers were milling about, unloading the provisions, setting up the stalls, getting prepared for the Saturday rush.

Jackson bore down on the congested scene without slackening speed. Behind him were yowling sirens and the red eyes of pursuing patrol cars.

162

"Look out!" a big colored man yelled.

Panicked people jumped for cover. A truck did the shimmy as the driver frantically steered one way and then the other trying to dodge the hearse.

When Jackson first noticed the congested market area, it was too late to stop. All he could do was try to put the hearse through whatever opening he saw. It was like trying to thread a fine needle with a heavy piece of string.

He bent to the right to avoid the truck, hit a stack of egg crates, saw a molten stream of yellow yolks filled with splinters splash past his far window.

The right wheels of the hearse had gone up over the curb and plowed through crates of vegetables, showering the fleeing men and the store fronts with smashed cabbages, flakes of spinach, squashed potatoes and bananas. Onions peppered the air like cannon shot.

"Runaway hearse! Runaway hearse!" voices screamed.

The hearse ran into crates of iced fish spread out on the sidewalk, skidded with a heavy lurch, and veered against the side of the refrigerator truck. The back doors were flung wide and the throat-cut corpse came one-third out. The gory head hung down from the cut throat to stare at the scene of devastation from its unblinking white-walled eyes.

Exclamations in seven languages were heard.

Caroming from the refrigerator truck, the hearse wobbled wildly to the other side of the street, climbed over a side of beef a delivery man had dropped to the street to run, and tore, staggering, down the street.

He was through the market area so fast a colored laborer exclaimed in a happy voice, "God damn, that was sudden!"

"But did you see what I seen?"

"You reckon he stole it?"

"Must have, man. What else the cops chasing him for?"

"What's he gonna do with it?"

"Sell it, man, sell it. You can sell anything in Harlem."

When the hearse came into the open at 100th Street, it was splattered with eggs, stained with vegetables, spotted

163

with blood. Chunks of raw meat, fish scales, fruit skins clung to the dented fenders. The back doors swung open and shut.

It had gained on the patrol cars, which had had to slow down in the market area. Jackson had the feeling of sitting in the middle of a nightmare. He was sealed in panic and he couldn't get out. He couldn't think. He didn't know where he was going, didn't know what he was doing. Just driving, that's all. He had forgotten why he was running. Just running. He felt like just sitting there behind the wheel and driving that hearse off the edge of the world.

He went through Puerto Rican Harlem at ninety miles an hour. An old Puerto Rican woman watched the hearse pass, saw the back doors swing open, and fainted dead away.

A patrol car screaming north on Park Avenue spotted the hearse coming south as it approached the intersection of 95th Street. The patrol car made a crying left turn. Jackson saw it and bent the big hearse in a long right turn. The back doors flew open and the corpse slid out slowly, like a body being lowered into the sea, thumped gently onto the pavement and rolled onto its side.

The patrol car swerved, trying to keep from running over it, went out of control and spun like a top on the wet street, bounced over the curb, knocked over a mailbox, and shattered the plate-glass window of a beauty shop.

Jackson went along 95th Street to Fifth Avenue. When he saw the stone wall surrounding Central Park he realized he was out of Harlem. He was down in the white world with no place to go, no place to hide his woman's gold ore, no place to hide himself. He was going at seventy miles an hour and there was a stone wall ahead.

His mind began to think. Thought rolled back on the lines of a spiritual:

> Sometimes I feel like a motherless child,
> Sometimes I feel like I'm almost gone . . .

Nothing left now but to pray.

He was going so fast that when he turned sharply north

on Fifth Avenue, heading back toward Harlem, the trunk slid back, went off the end of the coffin rack, bounced on the floor of the hearse, somersaulted into the street, landed on the bottom edge and burst wide open.

Jackson was so deep in prayer he didn't notice it.

He drove straight up Fifth Avenue to 110th Street, turned over to Seventh Avenue, kept north to 139th Street, and drew up in front of his minister's house.

He passed three patrol cars on the way. The cops gave the battered, dirty, meat-smeared, egg-stained hearse a cursory look and let it pass. No steamer trunks and dead bodies in that wreck. Jackson didn't even notice the patrol cars.

He parked in front of his minister's house, got out and went around to the back to lock the doors. When he found the hearse empty, that was the bitter end. Nothing even left to pray for. His girl was gone. Her gold ore was gone. His brother was dead, and gone too. He just wanted to throw himself on the mercy of the Lord. It was all he could do to keep from weeping.

Reverend Gaines was in the middle of a big religious dream when his housekeeper awakened him.

"Brother Jackson is downstairs in the study and says he wants to see you on something very important."

"Jackson?" Reverend Gaines exclaimed in extreme irritation, rubbing the sleep from his eyes. "You mean our brother Jackson?"

"Yes sir," that patient colored woman said. "Your Jackson."

"Lord save us from squares," Reverend Gaines muttered to himself as he got up to slip his black silk brocaded robe over his purple silk pyjamas, and descend to the study.

"Brother Jackson, what brings you to the house of the shepherd of the Lord at this ungodly hour, when all the other Lord's sheep are sleeping peacefully in the meadows?" he asked pointedly.

"I've sinned, Reverend Gaines."

165

Reverend Gaines stiffened as though someone had uttered blasphemy in his presence.

"Sinned! Good Lord, Brother Jackson, is that sufficient reason to awaken me at this hour of night? Who hasn't sinned? I was just standing on the banks of the River Jordon, dressed in a flowing white robe, converting sinners by the thousands."

Jackson stared at him. "Here in the house?"

"In a dream, Brother Jackson, in a dream," the minister explained, unbending enough to smile.

"Oh, I'm sorry I woke you up, but it's an emergency."

"That's all right, Brother Jackson, sit down." He sat down himself and poured a glass of liqueur from a cut-glass decanter on his mahogany desk. "Just a little elderberry cordial to awaken my spirit. Will you have a glass?"

"No sir, thank you," Jackson declined as he sat down facing Reverend Gaines across the desk. "My spirit is already wide awake as it is."

"You're in trouble again? Or is it the same trouble? Woman trouble, wasn't it?"

"No sir, it was about money the last time. I was trying to keep it from looking as if I had stolen some money. But this time it's worse. It's about my woman too. I'm in deep trouble this time."

"Has your woman left you? At last? Because you didn't steal the money? Or because you did?"

"No sir, it's nothing like that. She's gone but she hasn't left me."

Reverend Gaines took another sip of cordial. He enjoyed solving domestic mysteries.

"Let us kneel and pray for her safe return."

Jackson was on his knees before the minister was.

"Yes sir, but I want to confess first."

"Confess!" Reverend Gaines had started to kneel but he straightened up suddenly like a Jack-in-the-box. "You haven't killed the woman, Brother Jackson?"

"No sir, it's nothing like that."

Reverend Gaines gave a sigh of relief and relaxed.

166

"But I've lost her trunk full of gold ore."

"What?" Reverend Gaines's eyebrows shot upward. "Her trunk full of gold ore? Do you mean to say she had a trunk full of gold ore and never told me, her minister? Brother Jackson, you had better make a full confession."

"Yes sir, that's what I want to do."

At first, as Jackson unfolded the story of being swindled on The Blow and stealing five hundred dollars from Mr. Clay's to bribe the bogus marshal and trying to get even by gambling, Reverend Gaines was filled with compassion.

"The Lord is merciful, Brother Jackson," he said consolingly. "And if Mr. Clay is half as merciful, you will be able to work off that account. I will telephone to him about the matter. But what about this trunk full of gold ore?"

But when Jackson described the trunk and related how the gang had kidnapped his woman to get possession of it, Reverend Gaines's eyes began to widen with curiosity.

"You mean to say that that big green steamer trunk in that little room where you and she lived was filled with gold ore?"

"Yes sir. Pure eighteen-carat gold ore. But it didn't belong to her. It belonged to her husband and she had to give it back. So I had to get my brother, Goldy, to help me find them."

Revulsion replaced the curiosity in Reverend Gaines's eyes as Jackson described Goldy.

"You mean to say that Sister Gabriel was a man? Your twin brother? And he swindled our poor gullible people with tickets to heaven?"

"Yes sir, lots of people believed in them. But the only reason I went to him was because he was a crook and I needed him to help me."

As Jackson related the events of the night, Reverend Gaines's eyes got wider and wider, and horror began replacing the expression of revulsion. By the time Jackson got to his escape from the police at the 125th Street Station, Reverend Gaines was sitting forward on the edge of his seat with his mouth hanging open and his eyes

167

bulging. But Jackson had related the story as he had seen it happen, and Reverend Gaines did not understand why he had fled from the police.

"Was it because of your brother?" he asked. "Did they discover he was impersonating a nun?"

"No sir, it wasn't that. It was because he was dead."

"Dead!" Reverend Gaines jumped as though a wasp had stung him in the rear. "Great God above!"

"Hank and Jodie had cut his throat when I went upstairs to look for Imabelle."

"Good God, man, why didn't you call for help? Didn't you hear his cries?"

"No sir. I had sat down to rest for a minute and I had fell asleep."

"Merciful heavens, man! You fell asleep while you were looking for your woman who was in grave danger. While her fortune was sitting unprotected in that street—that street too, the most dangerous street in Harlem—protected only by your brother, a foul sinner who was scarcely better than a murderer himself." Reverend Gaines's rich black skin was turning gray at the very thought of what had happened. "And they cut his throat? And put his body in the hearse?"

Jackson mopped the sweat from his eyes and face.

"Yes sir. But I didn't mean to go to sleep."

"And what did you do with the hearse? Drive it off into the Harlem River?"

"No sir, it's parked out front."

"Out front! In front of my house?"

Forgetting his ecclesiastical dignity, Reverend Gaines jumped to his feet and shambled hastily across the room to peer through the front window at the battered hearse parked at the curb in the gray dawn. When he turned back to face Jackson he looked as if he had aged twenty years. His implacable self-confidence was shaken to the core. As he shuffled slowly back to his seat, his silk brocade robe flopped open and the pants of his purple silk pyjamas began slipping down. But he paid no attention.

"Do you mean to sit there, Brother Jackson, and tell me

that your brother's body with its throat cut and your woman's trunk full of gold ore are in that hearse out there, parked in front of my house?" he asked in horror.

"No sir. I lost them. They fell out somewhere, I don't know where."

"They fell out of the hearse? Into the street?"

"It must have been in the street. I didn't drive anywhere else."

"Just why did you come here, Brother Jackson? Why did you come to me?"

"I just wanted to kneel here beside you, Reverend Gaines, and give myself up to the Lord."

"What!" Reverend Gaines started as though Jackson had uttered blasphemy. "Give yourself up to the Lord? Jesus Christ, man, what do you take the Lord for? You have to go and give yourself up to the police. The Lord won't get you out of that kind of mess."

CHAPTER 23

THE RAYS of the rising sun over the Harlem River shone blood-red on the top floor of the building where Billie ran her after-hours joint.

"Can't I just wait in the car?" Imabelle asked. She was having trouble with her breathing.

"Get out," Grave Digger said flatly.

"What do you need me for? They're up there, I tell you. You know I can't run anywhere with these handcuffs on."

He saw that she was scared. She was trembling all over.

"Well, Little Sister, if it's your grave, just remember that you dug it," he said without mercy. "If Ed was here to see you I'd let you stay."

She got out, stumbling as her legs buckled. Grave Digger came around from the other side, took her by the arm, steered her up a flight of concrete stairs, through the glass double-doors, into a small immaculate foyer furnished with a long table, polished chairs and parchment-shaded lights flanking wall mirrors.

Not a sound could be hard.

"These slick hustlers live high on the hog," he muttered. "But at least they're quiet."

They rode in a push-button elevator to the sixth floor, and turned toward the jade-green door at the left of a square hall.

"I beg you," Imabelle pleaded, trembling.

"Go ahead and buzz her," Grave Digger ordered, flattening himself against the wall beside the door and drawing his long-barreled nickel-plated pistol.

She pushed the button. After a time the Judas window clicked open.

"Oh, it's you, honey," said a deep feminine voice, strangely pleasant.

The door was unlocked.

Grave Digger held his .38 in his right hand, put his left hand on the doorknob, and rode it in.

A vague shape in the almost pitch-dark hall moved slowly to one side to let him enter, and the deep voice said to Imabelle, not so pleasantly, "Well, come on inside and shut the door."

Imabelle pushed in behind Grave Digger, and the front of the dark hall was crowded. The faint sound of her teeth chattering could be heard in the silence.

The woman closed the door and locked it without speaking.

"You got some friends I want, Billie," Grave Digger said.

"Come into my office a moment, Digger."

She unlocked the first door to the left with a Yale key attached to a chain about her neck. A copper-shaded lamp spilled a soft glow on a blond-oak writing desk. When she switched on the bright overhead light, a luxurious bedroom suite, planted in the deep pile of a vermilion rug, sprang into view. She quickly closed the door behind them.

Grave Digger searched the room with one quick glance, looked an instant longer at the knobs of the doors to the closet and bathroom, then moved out into the room so that Billie was a target against the hall door.

"Talk fast," he said. "It's getting late."

She was a brown-skinned woman in her middle forties, with a compact husky body filling a red gabardine dress. With a man's haircut and a smooth, thick, silky mustache, her face resembled that of a handsome man. But her body was a cross. The top two buttons of the dress were open, and between her two immense uplifted breasts was a thick growth of satiny black hair. When she talked a diamond flashed between her two front teeth.

She flicked a glance at Imabelle's swollen, purple-tinted cheek, across Imabelle's scared-sick eyes, and then gave her whole attention to Grave Digger.

"Don't take them in the house, Digger. I'll send them out."

"Are they all together?"

"All? There's only two here now. Hank and Jodie."

"Slim ought to be here too," Imabelle said in a breathless voice. Both Grave Digger and Billie turned to stare at her.

"Maybe he's out looking for me."

Billie looked away from her first. Grave Digger stared an instant longer. Then both turned back toward each other.

"I'll take those two," Grave Digger said.

"Not in the house, Digger. They're hopped to the gills and kill-happy. I've got two of my best girls with them."

"That's the chance you take running this kind of joint."

"I don't run it for free, you know. I pay like hell. And the captain promised me there wouldn't be any rumbles in here."

"Where are they?"

"The captain won't like it, Digger."

Grave Digger looked at her thoughtfully.

"Billie, they threw acid in Ed's eyes."

Billie shuddered.

"Listen, Digger, I'll set them up. I'll take them down to the foyer myself and hand them over to you with their hands full of air."

"You know goddamn well they don't intend to leave that way. They're planning on going over the roof and coming out of the house next door."

"All right. Listen. I'll trade you. I'll give you three purse-snatchers, a prowler you've been wanting for a long time—"

"It's getting late, Billie."

"—and the Wilson murderer. The one who killed the liquor-store man during that stickup last month."

172

"I'm going to come back for them. But I'll take these two now."

She turned quickly and pulled open a top bureau-drawer.

Grave Digger drew a bead on the middle of her spine.

She pulled the drawer clear out, threw it on the bed. It was filled evenly with stacks of brand-new twenty-dollar bills.

"There's five grand. It's yours."

He didn't look at the money.

"Where are they, Billie? There isn't much time."

"They're in the pad. But they've got themselves locked in and they won't open even for me."

"They'll open for her," Grave Digger said, nodding toward Imabelle.

Billie turned to stare at Imabelle.

Imabelle had turned a sour-cream yellow with blue-black half-moons beneath her dog-sick eyes. She was trembling like a leaf.

"Don't make me do it. Please don't make me do it."

Tears streamed down her face. She knelt on the floor, clutched Grave Digger about the legs.

"I'll do anything. I'll be your woman, or a circus girl—"

"Get up," Grave Digger said without mercy. "Get up, or I'll blast open the door, holding you in front of me as a shield."

She got to her feet like an old woman.

Billie looked at her without pity.

"You know Hank when you see him?" Imabelle asked Grave Digger, talking in gasps. "The one who threw the acid?"

"I'd know that bastard in hell."

"He's the one who's got the gun."

"Digger, for God's sake be careful," Billie pleaded. "They got two of my best young girls in there. Jeanie's only sixteen and she's with Jodie—"

"You're talking yourself out of business."

"—and Jodie's on a kill-crazy edge with that knife. And Carol's only nineteen herself."

"Let's just hope neither of their numbers comes up," Grave Digger said.

He turned to Imabelle. "Go down and knock on the door."

When they came out of the room, a white man came from the bathroom next door, buttoning his fly, gave them a drunken look, and staggered quietly back to the sitting room.

Imabelle went down the hall as to her death.

There were six rooms and a bath in the flat, the four bedrooms facing across the long center-hall, the bath between Billie's office and the small bedroom called the pad. The hall ran into a big front combination dining-sitting room with shaded windows overlooking both 155th Street and St. Nicholas Avenue; a small electrically equipped kitchen was to the right.

There was a jukebox playing softly at one end of the sitting room; two white men sat on divans with three colored girls. At the other end, toward the kitchen, two colored men and a colored woman sat at a large mahogany dining table eating fried chicken and potato salad. The lights were low, the air faintly tinted with incense.

In one of the bedrooms a white man and a colored girl lay embraced between sky-blue sheets. In another, five colored men played a nearly wordless game of stud poker in the smoke-filled air, drinking cold beer from bottles and eating sandwiches.

The pad had a door opening into the hall, and another on the side at the back which opened into one end of the kitchen. Both doors were locked, with the keys in the locks. There was a single window opening onto the landing of the fire escape, but it was hidden behind heavy drapes drawn over Venetian blinds.

Hank lay on a couch, dressed in his blue suit, his head propped on two sofa pillows. He was slowly puffing opium through a water pipe. The shallow bowl with the bubbling opium pill rested on a brazier on a glass-covered cocktail table. The smoke passed through a short curved stem, bubbled in a glass decanter half-filled with tepid water, was drawn through a long transparent plastic tube into the amber mouthpiece which Hank held loosely between slack lips.

His .38 automatic lay beside him, out of sight against the wall.

A young girl wearing a white blouse over full, ripened breasts and tight-fitting slacks sat on the green carpet, her knees drawn up and her head resting back against the sofa. She had a smooth seal-brown face, big staring eyes, and a wide-lipped, flower-like mouth.

Jodie sat across the room, on a green leather ottoman. His head was bent over almost inside of the speaker of a console combination as he listened to a Hot Lips Page recording of *Bottom Blues,* playing it over and over so low that the notes were heard distinctly only by his drug-sharpened sense of hearing.

A girl sat on the floor between his outstretched legs. She wore a lemon-yellow blouse over budding breasts, and Paisley slacks. She had an olive-skinned, heart-shaped face, long black lashes concealing dark-brown eyes, and a mouth too small for the thickness of the lips. Her head rested on Jodie's knee.

Jodie was staring over her head, lost in the blue music. He ran his left hand slowly back and forth over her crisp brown curls as though he liked the sensation. His right arm rested on his thigh and in his right hand he held the bone-handled switch-blade knife, snapping it open and shut.

"Don't you have another record?" Hank asked, as if from a great distance.

"I like this record."

"Doesn't it have another side?"

"I like this side."

Jodie started the record again. Hank looked dreamily at the ceiling.

"When are we going?" Jodie asked.

"As soon as it gets daylight."

Jodie stared at the dial of his wrist watch.

"It ought to be daylight now."

"Give it some time: Ain't no hurry."

175

"I want to be on the road. I'm getting nervous sitting around here."

"Wait awhile. Give it some time. Let some traffic get on the road. We don't want to be the only car leaving town with California plates."

"How the hell you know there's going to be any others?"

"Ohio plates, then. Illinois plates. Give it some time."

"I'm giving it some mother— time."

The record came to a stop. Jodie started it over again, bent his ear to the speaker, and clicked the knife open and shut.

"Stop clicking that knife," Hank said indifferently.

"I didn't know I was clicking it."

A hesitant knock sounded above the low-playing blues.

Hank stared dreamily at the locked door. Jodie stared tensely. The girls didn't look up.

"See who's there, Carol," Hank said to the girl beside him. She started to get up. "Just ask."

"Who is it?" she asked in a harsh, startling voice.

"Me. Imabelle."

Hank and Jodie kept staring at the locked door. The girls turned and stared at it also. No one answered.

"It's me, Imabelle. Let me in."

Hank reached down along his side and wrapped his fingers about the butt of the automatic. Jodie's knife clicked open.

"Who's with you?" Hank asked in a lazy voice.

"Nobody."

"Where's Billie?"

"She's here."

"Call her."

"Billie, Hank wants to talk to you."

"Hank?" Hank said. "Who's Hank?"

"Don't use that name," Billie said, then to Hank, "I'm here. What do you want?"

"Who's with Imabelle?"

"Nobody."

"Open the door a crack," Hank said to Carol.

She got up and crossed the room in a hip-swinging walk,

unlocked the door and opened it a crack. Hank had his automatic aimed at the crack.

Imabelle put her face in view.

"It's Imabelle," Carol said.

Billie pushed the door open wider and looked past Imabelle at Hank. "Do you want to see her?"

"Sure, let her come in," Hank said, putting the gun out of sight beside him.

Carol opened the door wide and Imabelle stepped into the room. She was so scared she was biting down vomit.

Hank and Jodie stared at her tear-streaked face and swollen, purple-tinted cheek.

"Close the door," Hank said dreamily.

Imabelle stepped to one side, and Grave Digger came out of the dark hall like an apparition coming up from the sea. He had a nickel-plated pistol in each hand.

"Straighten up," he said thickly.

"It's a mother— plant," Jodie grated.

Jodie had his left hand resting on Jeanie's curly head, his right hand extended, the knife open. With a sudden tight grip his left hand closed and he lifted the girl up from the floor by her hair, holding her in front of him as a shield, and put the sharp naked blade tight against her throat as he came violently to his feet.

The girl didn't cry out, didn't utter a sound, didn't faint. Her body went flaccid beneath Jodie's grip. Her face was stretched into distortion, a drop of blood trickled slowly down her taut neck. Her eyes were huge black pools of animal terror, slanting upward at the edges, overwhelming her small distorted face. She didn't breathe.

Grave Digger caught a look at her face from the corner of his eye, and didn't move for fear of starting that knife across her throat.

Hank stared at Grave Digger dreamily without moving, his fingers still curled about the butt of the hidden .38. Grave Digger stared back. They were watching the flicker of each other's eyes, paying no attention to Jodie and the paralyzed girl. Nobody spoke. Carol stood frozen with one hand on the door knob. Imabelle stood trembling, out of range on the other side. Everything was in pantomime.

Jodie backed toward the door that opened into the kitchen. The girl backed with him, followed his every motion with a corresponding motion, as if performing some macabre dance. Her eyes were fixed straight ahead in pools of undripping tears.

Jodie brought up against the door. "Reach around me and open it," he ordered the girl.

The girl reached her left hand carefully around his body, felt for the key, turned it, and opened the door.

Jodie backed into the kitchen, still holding the girl in front of him.

Billie stood silently beside the white enamel electric range with a double-bladed wood-chopper's axe held poised over her right shoulder, waiting for Jodie to come into reach. He took another step backward, his eyes on Grave Digger's guns. Billie chopped his upper forearm in a forward-moving stroke to knock the knife blade forward from the girl's throat. Jodie wheeled in violent reflex his knife-arm flopping like an empty sleeve, as the knife clattered on the tiled floor, struck out backwards with the edge of his left hand. Billie took the blow across the mouth as she chopped him in the center of the back between the shoulder blades, like splitting a log, knocking him forward to his knees.

His head flew about to look at her as he cried, "Mother-raping—"

She put her whole weight in a down-chopping blow and sank the sharp blade of the axe into the side of his neck with such force it hewed through the spinal column and left his head dangling over his left shoulder on a thin strip of flesh, the epithet still on his lips.

Blood geysered from red stump of neck over the fainting girl as Billie dropped the axe, picked her bodily in her arms, and showered her with kisses.

As if it were a signal Hank was waiting for, he swung up the black snout of his .38 automatic, knowing that he didn't have a chance.

Before it had cleared his hip, Grave Digger shot him

through the right eye with his own pistol held in his right hand. While Hank's body was jerking from the bullet in the brain, Grave Digger said, "For you, Ed," took dead aim with Coffin Ed's pistol held in his left hand, and shot the dying killer through the staring left eye.

Pandemonium broke loose in the house. Imabelle slipped beneath Grave Digger's arm and bolted toward the door. Guests poured from the rooms into the narrow hall in a panic-stricken stampede.

But Grave Digger had already wheeled into the hall after Imabelle, pushed her into the corner, and blocked the door. He flicked on the bright overhead lights with the barrel of one gun and stood with his back against the door with a gun in each hand.

"Straighten up," he shouted in a big loud voice. And then, as if echoing his own voice, he mimicked Coffin Ed, "Count off."

"And now, Little Sister," he said to the cowering woman in the corner. "Where's Slim?"

Her teeth were chattering so she could scarcely speak.

"In the—in the trunk," she stammered.

CHAPTER 24

IT WAS HOT in the small room high up on the twenty-second floor of the granite-faced county building far downtown in City Center. Pink-shirted young Assistant DA John Lawrence, who had been assigned to conduct the interrogation, sat behind a large flat-topped green steel desk, his blond crew-cut hair shining with cleanliness in the slanting rays of the afternoon sun.

Jackson sat on the edge of a green leather chair across from him, dirty and disheveled and shades blacker than he ever looked in Harlem. Grave Digger sat sidewise on the wide window ledge, looking across Manhattan Island at an ocean liner going down the Hudson River, headed for the Narrows and Le Havre. A court stenographer sat at the end of the desk with a stylo poised over his notebook.

For a moment motion was suspended.

Lawrence had just finished questioning Jackson. Suddenly he stirred. He wiped the sweat from his freckled face, combed his manicured fingernails through his hair, and shifted his athletic shoulders in the Brooks Brothers gray flannel suit.

He had read Grave Digger's report over twice before he had begun his interrogation. He had read the report from the 95th Street precinct. The trunk containing Slim's body had been reported by a Fifth Avenue bus driver who had noticed it lying open in the street. The police had found Slim's body, bearing twenty stab-wounds, wrapped in a blanket weighted with rocks, and had taken it to the morgue.

The bodies of Hank and Jodie had also been taken to the

morgue. They had been identified by fingerprints as the men wanted in Mississippi for murder.

The apartment on Upper Park Avenue had been investigated. All it had revealed as evidence had been a quantity of fool's gold piled on the coal in the coalbin.

He had listened for two hours to the unfolding of the saga of the high-yellow woman and the trunk full of solid gold ore with increasing stupefaction. Still he did not believe he had heard it all correctly.

He stared at Jackson with a look of awed incredulity.

"Whew!" he whistled softly.

He and the court stenographer exchanged glances.

Grave Digger didn't look around.

"Any questions you want to ask, Jones?" Lawrence asked with a note of appeal.

Grave Digger turned his head.

"What for?"

Lawrence looked back at Jackson and said helplessly, "And you insist, to the best of your knowledge, that the trunk contained gold ore and nothing else?"

Jackson mopped his own shining black face with a handkerchief almost the same color.

"Yes sir, I'd swear to it on a stack of Bibles. As many times as I have seen it."

"You also state, to the best of your knowledge, that the Perkins woman had already left the scene—the area— when your brother—" He consulted his notes. "—er, Sister Gabriel, was murdered."

"Yes sir. I'd swear to it. I had looked all over for her and she was gone."

Lawrence cleared his throat.

"Had gone, yes. And you still contend that she—the Perkins woman, was held by this gang—this man Slim—against her will."

"I know she was," Jackson declared.

"How can you be so certain about that, Jackson? Did she tell you that?"

"She didn't have to tell me, Mr. Lawrence. I know she was. I know Imabelle. I know she wouldn't have taken up with those people without their making her. I know my Imabelle. She wouldn't do anything like that. I'd swear to it."

Grave Digger kept looking at the river.

Lawrence studied Jackson covertly, pretending he was reading his notes. He had heard of gullible colored people like Jackson, but he had never seen one in the flesh before.

"Ahem! And you insist that she had nothing to do with the gang's cheating you out of your money?"

"No sir. Why would she do that? It was as much her money as it was mine."

Lawrence sighed. "I don't suppose there's any need of asking, but it's a matter of form. You don't want to prefer charges against her, do you?"

"Prefer charges against her? Against Imabelle? What for, Mr. Lawrence? What's she done?"

Lawrence closed his notebook decisively and looked over at Grave Digger. "What's city got on him, Jones?"

Grave Digger turned back, but still didn't look at Jackson.

"Reckless driving. Destruction of property. Some of it is covered by the automobile insurance. And resisting arrest."

"Are you going to take him?"

Grave Digger shook his head. "His boss has already gone his bail."

Lawrence stared at Grave Digger.

"He has!" Jackson exclaimed involuntarily. "Mr. Clay? He's gone my bail? He hasn't got any warrant out for my arrest?"

Lawrence turned to stare at Jackson.

"He stole five hundred dollars from his boss," Grave Digger said. "Clay swore out a warrant for his arrest but late this morning he withdrew the charge."

Lawrence ran his fingers through his clipped hair again.

"All of these people sound as though they're raving crazy," he muttered, but when he noticed the stenographer taking down his words he said, "Never mind that." He looked at Grave Digger again. "What do you make of it?"

182

Grave Digger shrugged slightly. "Who knows?"

Lawrence stared at Jackson. "What have you got on your boss?"

Jackson fidgeted beneath the stare and mopped his face to hide his confusion. "I ain't got nothing on him."

"Shall I hold him as a material witness?" Lawrence appealed again to Grave Digger.

"What for? Witness against whom? He's told all he knows, and he's not going anywhere."

Lawrence let out his breath. "Well, you're free to go, Jackson. The county has nothing on you. But I advise you to contact all those claimants immediately—those people whose property you destroyed. Get them squared up before they press charges."

"Yes sir, I'm going to do that right away."

He stood up, then hesitated, fiddling with his chauffeur's cap.

"Have any of you-all heard anything from my woman —where she's at or anything?"

All three of them turned again to stare at him. Finally Lawrence said, "She's being held."

"She is? In jail? What for?"

They stared at him in an unbelieving manner. "We're holding her for questioning," Lawrence finally said.

"Can I see her? Talk to her, I mean?"

"Not now, Jackson. We haven't talked to her yet ourselves."

"When do you think I'll be able to see her?"

"Pretty soon, perhaps. You don't have to worry about her. She's safe. I advise you to get about squaring up those claimants as soon as you can."

"Yes sir. I'm going to see Mr. Clay right now."

When Jackson had left, Lawrence said to Grave Digger, "It's pretty well established that Jackson is as innocent as a lamb, don't you think?"

"Sheared lamb," the court stenographer put in.

Grave Digger grunted.

"Have you had any news on your partner, Jones?" Lawrence asked.

"I was by the hospital."

"How is he?"

"They said he would see, but he'd never look the same."

Lawrence sighed again, squared his shoulders and assumed a look of grim determination. He pressed a button on his desk, and when a cop poked his head in from the corridor, he said, "Bring in the Perkins woman."

Imabelle wore the same red dress, but now it looked bedraggled. The side of her face where Grave Digger had slapped her had flowered into deep purple streaked with orange.

She gave Grave Digger a quick look and shied away from his calculating stare. Then she took the seat facing Lawrence, started to cross her legs but thought better of it and sat with her knees pressed together, her back held rigid, on the very edge of the seat.

Lawrence looked at her briefly, then studied the notes in front of him. He took his time and reread all the reports.

"Jesus Christ, all this cutting and shooting," he muttered. "This room is swimming in blood. No, no, don't take that," he added to the court stenographer.

He looked up at Imabelle again, slowly stroking his chin, wondering where to begin questioning her.

"Who was Slim?" he finally asked. "What was his real name? We have him down here as Goldsmith. In Mississippi he was known as Skinner."

"Jimson."

"Jimson! Is that a name? Christian name or family name?"

"Clefus Jimson. That was his real name."

"And the other two. What were their real names?"

"I don't know. They used a lot of names. I don't know what their real names were."

"This Jimson." The name felt unpleasant in his mouth. "We'll just call him Slim. Who was Slim? What was your connection with him?"

"He was my husband."

"I thought as much. Where were you married?"

"We weren't exactly married. He was my common-law husband."

"Oh! Were you—did you keep in touch with him? That is, while you were living with Jackson?"

"No sir. I hadn't seen him or heard anything about him for almost a year."

"Then how did he get in touch with you—or you in touch with him, however it worked?"

"I ran into him at Billie's by accident."

"Billie's?" Lawrence consulted his notes again. "Oh yes, that's where the other two were killed." My God, the blood, he was thinking. "What were you doing at Billie's?"

"Just visiting. I'd go up there afternoons when Jackson was at work, just to sit around and visit. I didn't like to hang around in bars where it might cast reflections on him."

"Ah. I see. And when you met Slim you and he connived together to cheat Jackson on the confidence game—" He glanced at his notes. "The Blow."

"I didn't want to. They made me do it."

"How could they force you to do it if you didn't want to?"

"I was scared to death of him. All three of them. They had it in for me and I was scared they'd kill me."

"You mean they had a grudge against you. Why?"

"I'd taken the trunk full of gold ore they used to work their lost-gold-mine racket with."

"You mean the fool's gold that was found in the coalbin where you and Slim lived?"

"Yes sir."

"You took it when?"

"When I left him in Mississippi. He was playing around with another woman and when I left I just up and took it and brought it to New York. I knew they couldn't work the racket without it."

"I see. And when he found you at Billie's he threatened you."

"He didn't have to. He just said, 'I'm gonna take you

185

back and we're gonna rook that nigger you been living with.' Hank and Jodie was there too. Hank was all hopped up and in that mean dreamy way he has when he's hopped and Jodie was gaged on heroin and kept snapping that knife open and shut and looking at me as if he'd like to cut my throat. And Slim, he was half-drunk. And Hank said they were going to take the gold ore and start operating right here in New York. There wasn't nothing for me to say. I had to do it."

"All right. Then you contend that you participated under duress. That they forced you on threat of death to work with them in their racket?"

"Yes sir. It was either that or get my throat cut. There was no two ways about it."

"Why didn't you go to the police?"

"What could I say to the police? They hadn't done nothing then. And I didn't know they were wanted in Mississippi for murder. That happened after I'd gone."

"Why didn't you go to the police after they had cheated Jackson out of fifteen hundred dollars?"

"It was the same thing. I didn't know then that Jackson had got hep that he'd been beat. If I'd gone to the police then and Jackson hadn't preferred charges, the cops would have just let them go. And they'd have killed me then for sure. I didn't know then about Jackson's brother. I just knew that Jackson himself was a square and he couldn't help me none."

"All right. But why didn't you go to the police after they'd thrown acid into Detective Johnson's face?"

She glanced fleetingly in the direction of Grave Digger, and drew into herself. Grave Digger was staring at her with a fixed expression of hate.

"I didn't have any chance," she said in a pleading tone of voice. "I would have, but I couldn't. Slim was with me all the time until we got home. Then after Hank and Jodie came down the river in that motorboat they rented, they got out underneath the railroad bridge and came straight to the place where Slim and me was at. Then there wasn't any use of thinking about going."

186

"What happened there?"

Sweat filmed her bruised face beneath their concentrated stares.

"Well, you see, Jodie thought I'd ratted to the police, until Slim showed him where I couldn't have ratted. I hadn't never had no chance. Jodie was gaged and evil and if it hadn't been for Hank, Jodie and Slim would have got to fighting again. Hank was the only one carried a gun, and he put his gun on Jodie and stopped him. Then Jodie wanted him and Hank to take the gold ore and lam and leave me and Slim there. Slim said they couldn't take the gold ore without taking him and me too. Then Hank said he agreed with Jodie. They couldn't take Slim on account of the acid burns on his neck and face. The cops could identify him too easy. They'd put two and two together and know just who he was. Hank said for Slim to hole up somewhere until his face got healed and they'd send for him, but meantime they'd take the gold ore. Slim said nobody was taking his gold ore, he didn't give a damn what they did. Then before Hank could stop him Jodie had stuck him in the heart and kept on sticking him until Hank said, 'Let up, God damn it, or I'll kill you.' But by then Slim was dead."

"Where were you when all this was happening?"

"I was there, but I couldn't do nothing. I was scared to death that Jodie was going to start sticking me too. He would have if Hank hadn't stopped him. He was like a crazy man."

"But why did they put the body in the trunk?"

"They wanted to get rid of it to keep from having another murder rap hanging on them in New York. Hank said he knew where they could get some more fool's gold in California. So they just left enough in the trunk to weight it down and threw the rest in the coalbin. They were planning to drop the trunk into the Harlem River. Hank said he was going to get a truck to move it and Jodie was supposed to stand downstairs and keep on the lookout. I was supposed to scrub the blood off the floor. I was too scared to think about leaving with Jodie standing downstairs. I didn't know he had gone with Hank until Jackson and his brother came to take the trunk."

Lawrence rubbed his chin angrily, trying to get the picture into focus. His eyes seemed out of focus too.

"Just where did you fit into their plans?"

"They were going to take me with them. I was scared they were going to take me out and kill me on the road somewhere."

"But you had already gotten away by the time they returned and killed Goldy?"

"Yes sir. I didn't know anything about that."

"Why didn't you notify the police then?"

"I was planning to. I was going down to the police station and tell the first policeman I saw. But that man attacked me before I had even gotten there, and before I had a chance to say anything the police had rushed me off to jail for just trying to protect myself."

Lawrence paused to study the report again.

"I told Detective Jones where to find Hank and Jodie just as soon as I got a chance," she added.

Lawrence blew out a sighing breath. "But you induced your boy-friend, Jackson, and his brother—er, Sister Gabriel—to move the trunk containing Slim's body without telling them what was in it?"

"No sir, I didn't induce them. They had their minds made up to take it and I was afraid if I told them they'd stay there trying to get the gold ore and let Hank and Jodie come back and find them and there'd be more killing. I knew Jackson believed it was real gold ore and I could see his brother believed it too. I figured the best thing was to let them take the trunk and get away as fast as they could. Then they'd be gone before Hank and Jodie got back."

"You said that Jodie was standing downstairs as a lookout."

"That's what I thought at first, but when Jackson and his brother came upstairs I knew Jodie must have gone with Hank. I figured that after they'd gotten away safe I could

188

tell the police about everything and wouldn't anybody else get hurt."

Lawrence looked over at Grave Digger. "Do you believe that?"

"No. She saddled Jackson and Goldy with the body and planned to lam on the first train leaving town. She didn't give a damn what happened to any of them."

"I just didn't want to see anybody else get hurt," Imabelle protested. "There was enough people killed already."

"All right, all right," Lawrence said. "That's your story."

"It ain't no story. It's the truth. I was going to tell the police everything. But that big black mother— that man attacked me before I had a chance."

"All right, all right, you've told your story."

Lawrence turned to Grave Digger. "I'll hold her for complicity."

"What for? You can't convict her. She claims they forced her to do it. Jackson will support her contention. He believes it and she knows he believes it. It's proven they were dangerous men. Who's left to deny her story? All the witnesses against her are dead, and any jury you find will believe her."

Lawrence mopped his hot red face.

"How about yours and Johnson's testimony?"

"Let her go, let her go," Grave Digger said harshly. He looked as if he were riding the crest of a rage. "Ed and I will square accounts. We'll catch her uptown some day with her pants down."

"No, I can't have that," Lawrence said. "I'll hold her in five thousand dollars' bail."

CHAPTER 25

Mr. Clay was having his afternoon nap when Jackson arrived. Jackson found the front door open and walked in without knocking. Smitty, the other chauffeur, was whispering with a woman in the dimly lit chapel.

Jackson opened the door to Mr. Clay's office softly and entered quietly. Mr. Clay lay on the couch, facing the wall. Dressed in his tailcoat attire, his long bushy gray hair floating on the coverlet, parchment-like skin framed by the dark wall, he looked like a refugee from a museum, in the dim light from the floor lamp that burned continuously in the front window.

"That you, Marcus?" he asked suddenly without turning.

"No sir, it's me, Jackson."

"Have you got my money, Jackson?"

"No sir—"

"I didn't think so."

"But I'm going to pay you back every cent, Mr. Clay—that five hundred dollars I borrowed and that two hundred you advanced me on my salary. Don't you worry about that, Mr. Clay."

"I'm not worrying, Jackson. You can put in a claim against the county for the money those hoodlums swindled you out of."

"I can? Against the county?"

"Yes. They had eight thousand dollars in their possession. But just keep it to yourself, Jackson, just keep it to yourself."

"Yes sir, I'll certainly do that."

"And Jackson—"

"Yes sir?"

"Did you bring back my hearse?"

"No sir. I didn't know whether I could. I left it parked in front of the station house."

"Then go get it, Jackson. And hurry back, because there's work for you to do."

"You're going to take me back, Mr. Clay?"

"I haven't never let you go, Jackson. A good man like you is hard to find."

"Yes sirree. Will you bury my brother for me, Mr. Clay?"

"I'm in the business, Jackson. I'm in the business. How much insurance did he have?"

"I don't know yet."

"Find out then, Jackson, and we'll talk business."

"Yes sir."

"How's that yellow woman of yours, Jackson?"

"She's fine, Mr. Clay. But she's in jail right now."

"That's too bad, Jackson. But anyway, you know she ain't cheating on you."

Jackson forced a laugh. "You're always joking, Mr. Clay. You know she wouldn't do anything like that."

"Not as long as she's in jail, anyway," Mr. Clay said sleepily.

"I'm going down to try to see her now."

"All right, Jackson. See Joe Simpson and have him go her bail—if it's not too much."

"Yes sir. Thank you, Mr. Clay."

Joe Simpson had his office on Lenox Avenue, around the corner. Jackson rode with him back downtown to the county building.

When Assistant DA Lawrence learned that Imabelle was making bail, he sent for Joe Simpson. Grave Digger and the court stenographer had gone, and Lawrence was alone in his office.

"Joe, I want to know who's going that woman's bail?" he asked.

Simpson looked at him in surprise.

"Why, Mr. Clay is."

"Jesus Christ!" Lawrence exclaimed. "What is this? What's going on here? What have they got on him? They steal his money, wreck his hearse, take advantage of him in every way that's possible, and he hastens to go their bail to get them out of jail. I want to know why."

"Two of those fellows had eight thousand dollars on them when they were killed."

"What's that got to do with it?"

"Why, I thought you knew how that worked, Mr. Lawrence. The money goes for their burials. And Mr. Clay got their funerals. It's just like they've been drumming up business for him."

Jackson was in the other wing of the building, waiting in the vestibule, when the jailor brought Imabelle from her cell. He gave a long sighing laugh and took her in his arms. She wriggled closely against the curve of his fat stomach and welded her bruised lips against his sweaty kiss.

Then she drew back and said, "Daddy, we got to hurry and see that old buzzard and get our room back so we'll have somewhere to sleep tonight."

"It's going to be all right," he told her. "I got my job back. And it was Mr. Clay who went your bail."

She held him at arms' length and looked into his eyes.

"And you got your job back too, Daddy. Well ain't that fine?"

"Imabelle," he said sheepishly. "I just want to tell you, I'm sorry I lost your trunk full of gold ore. I did the best I could to save it."

She laughed out loud and squeezed his strong, fat arms.

"Daddy, don't you worry. Who cares about an old trunk full of gold ore, as long as I got you?"